A Kind and Forgiving Time

J. David Thayer

BookLocker
Trenton, Georgia

This little book is dedicated to anyone who has gone through the dying process with a loved one, to anyone who has suffered a horrific loss unexpectedly, and to people who lose their tempers, occasionally, while driving. It is also dedicated to people who find the holiday season a complicated blend of emotions nearly impossible to sort through. In other words, this little book is dedicated to pretty much everyone (sooner or later).

"I have always thought of Christmas as a good time; a kind, forgiving, charitable, pleasant time; the only time I know of when men and women seem by one consent to open their shut-up hearts freely and to think of people as if they really were fellow passengers to the grave, and not another race of creatures bound on other journeys..."

—Scrooge's Nephew, *A Christmas Carol*, Charles Dickens

A Saturday Morning in Mid-December

A few scattered vehicles amongst the collective were decorated for the holiday season to the enjoyment of some and to the annoyance of others and to the complete indifference of most. Otherwise this might have been any Saturday morning plucked from the calendar at random. This particular section of I-55 in Corsequette Louisiana never experienced relief from its congestion. Here I-65 came in from Baton Rouge and headed off towards Biloxi and Mobile and afterward turned northbound and eventually up to Indianapolis and beyond. Questionable planning from the onset and, once constructed, no remedies for certain gridlock were feasible. All travelers momentarily suffered here in unison and today was no exception.

The traffic merging across all three lanes was a knot of indecision. To the far right was the express lane and its $6.25 surcharge. For that drivers encountered fewer cars and fewer off-ramps and more opportunities to safely exceed the posted speed limit. The center lane was the exact same road allocated to the masses desiring to pay nothing additional for the usage of the interstate beyond their taxes and it was stunted by four times as many exits, none of which led to anywhere a person was likely to go. The commoners' lane was a clogged firehose of construction barriers and first responders and rubberneckers and generalized impatience. The lane to the far left was a hard veer into the downtown district and was thus essentially useless save for the occasional driver yet retaining an interest in the arts or local commerce or other tangible exchanges of culture.

Almost no vehicles chose to go either right or left and several drivers in the outer lanes arrived at their final decisions a bit later than others. Naturally these needed to merge back into the constipated center and ahead of the throng already mired in the clog for several dozens of angry seconds and pulling crap like this was in direct violation of numerous unwritten rules of the road. There are some things you just don't do. To discourage such outrage, center lane vehicles clung to the bumpers ahead of them in a passive aggressive phalanx of disproportionate righteous indignation. This far and no farther. We can wreck if that's where you wanna go. Call the tow truck and the adjusters and the cops. You ain't getting in here today. Some responded to this response by shoehorning their way into where the nonexistent gap should occur and thus battles of wills ensued. Pissing matches expelling exhaust and pollution. Backing down was tantamount to base cowardice. It was unacceptable to allow a fellow traveler to claim victory and therefore dominance even in a relationship whose entire lifespan would disappear in under seven seconds. One had to continue living with oneself. And Saturdays like today are happy days. Especially during the holidays.

It is impossible to know the mind of the driver next to you.

Even worse than the late lane-changer is the guy who invents his own lane altogether. Here comes this asshole driving up the shoulder as if the rest of the motionless cars are stalled there on purpose. You know what happens next. When he gets as far up the makeshift and illegal lane as he can go and comes across an embankment or a guardrail or an abandoned couch or a dead deer or a forced exit he will put on his left blinker and expect acceptance back into the fray. Of course the forty cars that saw the asshole pull this move will then fuse together in unified animosity. Let him stay stuck in his bad choice until his tank runs dry and he walks down the hill and into the urban nest of decay in utter shame seeking a gallon of fuel and a plastic can to carry it in. And then let him burn that as well without bettering his situation at all. This would be justice, but no. Some mindless sap will surely let him back in.

Someone up the line will eventually decide to be kind to this skidmark and in so doing screw everyone else behind him or her who were all doing exactly what they were supposed to do the whole time. Now this guy has managed to shave three minutes off his journey by being the asshole we already established him to be at the start of this same paragraph. And worse: his choice is now irrevocably validated, meaning he will pull this same crap again and at his next opportunity. Happens thousands of times every day across the webbing of highway covering the United States and it happens in this location way more often than should be its fair share. Someone somewhere should do something.

Today every driver in every separate vehicle felt the same thing to varying degrees. A sort of relentless pressure waring against grace and deference and even holiday spirit could not slake the tension. The stress of the week just ended lingering on or else the continuing stress for those working over the weekend or else the presence of the perpetually entitled who expect never to wait for anything under any circumstances and whose patience is always a membrane at the best of times. All of it working together in concert.

This bit of congestion, though comparatively minor and also very short in duration, summoned hate's ultimate muse on the regular. Curse the city planners and curse indecisive drivers and curse everyone in my way and why can't everyone be just like me and do exactly what I would do even though I have done the thing making me furious right now at other times to other people and screw them anyway. And Saturdays like today are happy days. Especially during the holidays.

He was messing with playlists on his smartphone plugged into the dedicated media port of his new black SUV. He was used to CDs. Also a new onboard GPS was now guiding him through a drive he had made twenty times in the last ten years without AI assistance.

Stop to pee or to eat a fried pie and his copilot would scold him to proceed to the route and he would obey. The tech was still new to him and he was trying to adapt. All he wanted was a compass on his review mirror because he gets lost easily and a whole bunch of other features that he did not understand were also piled into that package and now he was lost inside his own new vehicle. But maybe this trip was the right place to learn how to use everything. It made sense to at least try, considering he would continue paying for all of this extra crap for the next five to seven years or until he traded in this vehicle for something even better and also even worse.

This was the first leg of a road trip crossing over six states and more than 900 miles. He was headed north to see his mom. It would require two hard days of driving to get all the way from Louisiana to Chicago and the open road was just what he needed in more ways than one. His copier clients would have to wait and some would not want to wait and his boss would certainly want none of them to wait. Neither does transitioning to the dying process want to wait. One entity can't be bargained with and the other is terminal. He made a choice and so here he was. Lots to sort out both before and after. And during. Thinking never left him but thinking about his driving was a struggle. Always on autopilot unless some new adjustment suddenly became necessary. He was basically competent but he was not exactly safe at all times and he had thousands of brothers and sisters just like him filling up every roadway across the nation. Sometimes these siblings made him flush with anger and he never found this ironic.

He had created numerous playlists for this very road trip. Some were in excess of six hours played end to end. He even made a playlist of Christmas music but he never cued it up. Seemed like a good idea, but yuck. Had this trip occurred during the week the driver would still be listening to the radio. He would have preferred to listen to his local sports station in Baton Rouge until he progressed out from underneath its broadcast radius but this was a Saturday morning. Instead of the usual slate of programming, he was treated to two hours of golf talk and he was not a golfer. He liked the weekday morning guys especially because they only used sports talk as an excuse to talk about literally anything else, including farts. Giggle. The weekend was a different story. Nothing is less interesting to a non-golfer than golf talk so he had to dip into his audio streaming account sooner than expected. But which playlist? What was he in the mood for? No. No. Not that. That's a good one but not yet. Maybe in Missouri. This one I guess. Why is this so hard? They were fun to build but he was already bored and so far he had not begun playing even one.

At the interstate juncture previously described traffic in all three lanes often stopped altogether. If only momentarily. He joins our story exactly in this spot. Dead stops all around. The man in the black SUV looked up from trying to navigate his loathsome media interface and noticed he was in the right lane which was the wrong lane. The right lane was the express lane and he had no use for the express lane. Where's the logic in paying extra to save yourself a few minutes when you have 870 miles yet ahead of you? But now he was committed and stuck and the angry horde occupying the choice center was resolute against his reentry. What could he do? Pay the needless toll or make something happen? Then his opportunity presented itself.

The portion of the road where he was at standstill was on a steep incline. In the desired lane and directly on his left was a white dually pulling a trailer. It was filled with all sorts of household furnishings and sundry belongings and the truck bed was also full. Blue polyethylene tarps stretched across both payloads and tied with bungee cables but not very secure in either case, flapping in the breeze even while motionless. He knew that once traffic cleared his peppy new black SUV would respond quicker than a dually pulling a trailer uphill and so he waited. Maybe five seconds. Both lanes got the same bit of separation at about the same time and he jumped lanes as soon as he saw a sufficient gap to do so. There was never any question as to whether he had enough room. He certainly did. However this could have been construed as a dick move and it was. The man in the white dually laid onto his horn. Three full seconds worth. The driver of the black SUV felt this was an exaggerated reaction and he looked up into his rearview mirror ready to receive the bird, but the driver in the white dually did not offer him one. Instead he had simply blown his horn and thus had had his say. Okay. Fair enough. You win. Sorry pal. My bad. Lot on my mind today.

The man in the black SUV returned his thoughts to every cross-purposed meat hook pulling separately on his brain and relegated the task of driving back to his subconsciousness reflexes coupled with muscle memory. The open road lay ahead, mostly straight and effectively endless and somehow peaceful. He set his cruise control for three miles above the speed limit and he completely disconnected his brain from monitoring his driving habits, and why not? He could still jerk the wheel if he had to.

You should leave a job when you have lost your passion for doing it. This is certainly wisdom. During his career many eminent speakers had spewed forth similar sage pablum at motivational conferences and in launch meetings and on podcasts and in required book studies and most recently over virtual meetings and he had always agreed with this basic sentiment. However his bills and his commitments and his 401K had not agreed with any such high ground piety and so, even though he now found himself matching that description, he continued working anyway. Who leaves his family in financial ruin simply because he isn't feeling it anymore?

None of the motivational speakers ever seemed to address this question.

Bluetooth calls about things he could no longer make himself care about would happen on the highway somewhere up the road and maybe even later from inside his motel room. But not yet. Only when such calls could be put off no longer. For now the agenda was whatever playlist sounded the least bothersome and glazed eyes fixed vaguely ahead and the relinquishing of his mind to old memories mingled with sadness and joy and also mingled with other things.

He knew his family was proud of him and he was happy and he was exhausted and this was fine because not everyone could say as much. He liked being that man but this trip wasn't about any of that. He was leaving that world and returning to a sketchy old nest built of haggard and complicated roots and twigs. All those old dynamics yet ruled that old nest and nothing about his adult life had any influence over it. He wasn't sure what his mom thought about the man he had become and suddenly that validation carried a lot more weight than it did even a month ago. He wondered whether he was a good son or a bad son. Some things simply have no metric for objective measurement.

He noticed traffic was lighter in this spot. Big exhale. He was glad about that. He decided to scan the bandwidth for an overly chatty DJ because that sort of DJ could almost pass for company for maybe an hour or so. Even golf talk would be okay now but he was too late for that.

A White Dually on an Incline

Everything he owned was in his truck bed and stacked onto his trailer. He couldn't continue paying for the storage unit and he had emptied its contents when the gates opened on this particular Saturday morning during the holiday season. The leasing agent had informed him that by Monday his unit would be sold at auction like you see on television and a horrid group of opportunistic vultures would pick and peck over the remnant of his ruined life for whatever silver coins they might salvage in the resale market. He imagined what might have been visible to this hypothetical assembly of pawnshop pirates gathered round the opening of his unit and the man doubted his few mean sticks of furniture would inspire any sort of serious bidding exchange. Likely the sale price would be less than the cost of a month's rent for that same unit when empty. A lot less. But none of that mattered. He needed his things. At least he assumed he would need them eventually. Might even need the padlock. Don't let them cut it! But none of that was true and he knew it.

Set fire to the lot of it and he could not have cared less. Somehow he just could not let it end this way. Don't let them win, even in defeat. He had lost enough already. Retreat if you must but show your fangs doing it. This is your story so make sure you're the one doing the telling. Even if the journey terminated at a local dump somewhere up I-55 and he had to offload everything he once treasured into a tangled pile just ahead of a bulldozer waiting to cover the last of his memories with topsoil and seagulls circling overhead ready to cover even that with their white shit and their endless peels of squawk! squawk! squawk! at least all of this would be on his own terms. There was dignity in choosing your own Waterloo and in setting your own appointment for arrival. Making them wait on you. He told himself all sorts of things that he did not believe and things that would have made no real difference to him even if he had believed them. But he had to tell himself something. Otherwise the noise inside his skull would return and deafen him and he hated the things the noise would say.

He was now ready to leave. There was nowhere to go.

What the leasing agent did not know was that this timing was not accidental. It had been a year since he had first moved into his basement flat below the shuttered bookstore and now that lease was up as well. About two years had passed since the tragedy and that felt like a lifetime ago. Which it was. It was also just yesterday. Brite Star Staffing Service had run out of short-term gigs for drywallers for the foreseeable future and what they were offering instead was not going to pay enough to live on. Not even for the kind of living he was reduced to these days. The good news was he saw all of this coming several months before the hammers would undoubtedly begin to fall and he started saving his paychecks instead of paying his bills. Fuck em. Desperation has both a ceiling and a floor and at some point he hit one of the two or both of them. And here it finally occurred to him: why am I staying here? In Corsequette, I mean? It was the closest thing to peace he had felt in two years and he almost did not recognize the sensation when it arrived. An old friend on your porch with extra weight and a long gray beard and the two of you have not exchanged a word in a decade. But there Peace was, standing right in front of him, and he brought with him an answer. Not a complete answer but an answer nonetheless.

All of it had happened right here in this awful town. So get out. Why not just get out? In fact why not leave Louisiana altogether? What was going to change? What was left to discover or to understand? What was left to try that he had not tried already? Suddenly he understood this much at least: everything he saw everywhere in Corsequette sickened him. This town. This damn town. It was all part of the same thing. Somehow the decaying downtown district and the various neighborhoods spiraling outwards and even its laughable quasi-suburbs of bourgeois pukey newbuild were mocking him and subjecting him to open shame. How many of those new homes out in the faux burbs had he helped to build over the last decade and where was the gratitude? Who came to the rescue when he lost his house? This damn town didn't care about his sweat or his blood or his bent back or his ruined family and it was even worse than that. The apathy was spiked with animosity. It was alive, this town, and it hated him. In fact, they hated each other. And this was convenient because he was on borrowed time either way. His situation was untenable no matter how he felt about this town.

Suppose he continued ignoring his situation and took no action at all. He could keep paying for his storage unit and his cheap basement flat for maybe one or two more months but that would be it. Meanwhile he could continue bouncing around to whatever job needed maybe two or three weeks of minimum wage grunt work and then what? Hold up a cardboard sign before an overpass? There was no way he would be in a position to sign on for another year of lease payments and there was no reason to even try. Clarity. Why not get ahead of it? He dug out his lease agreements and paid particular attention to the sections on eviction procedures and he knew he had them. He discovered exactly how long it would take for them to have enough grounds to throw him out of his basement and out of his unit and from there he counted backwards and drew a circle on his calendar. After this day they don't get one more crying dime! By the time they want me out I'll have a decent stack of cash and I'll be ready to leave Corsequette anyway. Just watch. Watch what I do next.

For the first time in two years things had actually played out the way he had predicted. More or less. Only he didn't follow through with punching his landlord across the jaw while handing in his keys like he had imagined himself doing many times leading up to today. Keys in the left and then a right cross. Teeth spraying everywhere and blood and spit and astonishment. He skipped this step because then there would be warrants and handcuffs and appearances and depositions and public defenders and court costs and maybe fines and maybe community service and maybe even time in county and certainly delays and the eventual upshot of all of it would be less cash to work with once he reached the other side. Wherever that turned out to be. And then a new job worth having would be even harder to find. Deep breaths. Damn he wanted to punch him though. But sometimes you have to lose and sometimes you just have to take it.

Down in the parking garage he hitched his trailer to his white dually and he climbed inside behind the steering wheel. And he punched his dashboard instead as a proxy for his landlord and for all of it and he did so repeatedly. He yelled and he cursed and the landlord had little to do with any of it. To be fair the man owning the white dually was intentionally late on his rent by three months and why should he expect his landlord to be anything other than an ass about that? But blaming his landlord worked well enough and fairness is not a mandate so the man had his villain. If he were making a list the landlord's name would have been on it. But he was not making lists today. This morning was about new beginnings. Today was about a fresh start.

He drove up from the parking garage and he headed off towards the storage yard. And then he began emptying the unit into whatever boxes and bins he could scrounge up ahead of time. When he ran out of those he piled the rest of his belongings loosely into the trailer and the truck bed as best he could. On one box was written the words X-Mas Decorations in black marker and it broke his heart remembering what was likely inside. Suddenly he realized his belongings weren't junk at all. In fact this stuff was all he had left connecting his life to their lives. To that time. These random items were a collective memory taking on physical form. He put that box inside the cab of his truck. It would be safer in there. Once the unit was empty he draped blue tarps over both loads and strapped them down with bungee cables and in completing the task he felt a lying sensation of satisfaction.

His trailer was filled with his old life and so was his truck bed because screw those bastards. They can't have anything that belongs to me even if it is garbage. He was surprised by how much his remaining junk had weighed down his old rig. Truck and trailer riding a bit lower now. Must be the old appliances, none of which were worth dragging around with him. Except for maybe his cast-iron potbelly pellet stove. Fairly new still. Heavy son of a gun! Somehow he had managed to load everything by himself using odd combinations of several types of dollies. This was hardly his first solo move.

Besides his personal effects he had upwards of four grand in folding cash stuffed inside his glovebox. Nothing else was in there except his proof of insurance and his registration and a snubnose .357 that he had originally purchased for home protection. Took some classes before he bought it and did some research. Got his permit eventually. Half a box of rounds in the glovebox also.

The onramp to I-55 was two lights east of the storage lot. This had been a vague notion occupying his imaginings for some time. Follow the open road wherever it leads. Fun to think about and also wildly impractical. Before putting his truck in gear it only made sense to finally settle on a heading at the very least. One onramp pointed north and the other pointed south. He thought about it. When you have no destination one way is as good as another. But head south from Corsequette for very long and you soon hit the Gulf. He had spent plenty of time down there already. Blackened redfish and blackened speckled trout and boiled crawdads with little ears of corn and so much good eating but not much else. To the north were so many places and he had never seen any of them. Memphis. St. Louis. Chicago. The Twin Cities and Canada after that. Canada is always looking for transplanted Americans with American dollars seeking to leave their checkered pasts behind and start over and with never an indiscrete question asked. Canadians love Americans and every American knows this. Maybe his next life was somewhere in Canada and maybe it was somewhere else. In either case heading north was certainly the better choice. Obviously. Things would work out if he just headed north long enough to discover wherever he was supposed to be. A new year two weeks away and his past behind him forever by then. He told himself all sorts of things and his own lies conspired with him and comforted him and he left the storage yard and Corsequette Louisiana forever.

He turned left underneath the overpass and merged onto I-55 North. The noise was coming back. Why now? For the first time in forever we were doing something positive. This was positive. We were leaving the old life behind us and all of its baggage and all of its sorrow and all of its grief and all of its regret and soon we will be outside the city limits and this awful town will lose its grip on us forever. No it won't. Yes it will. You will see. It never was the town. Shut up. Of course it was. You know better. No. You will see. Things will be better up north. Nothing will ever be better. You'll still be with you when you get to wherever you're going. Yes it will be better now hush up. You will see. Hush up. I said hush up you will see.

He drove north and he argued with himself mentally and audibly until the noise finally fell silent again and he experienced an uneasy armistice of the mind. Nothing more lasting than the chartable ebb of a relentless and angry tide. But it was okay now.

He was glad to be driving. He liked driving and he was good at it. Probably could have made a decent career out of it but he had made other choices. Maybe he should look into it now. He thought about it. He took heart in imagining that everything imaginable including what was formerly ridiculous was now suddenly possible. Dreaming is free and dreaming is typically harmless so why not?

He thought about how the road has its own set of rules. Not the laws. Everyone knows the laws. You can't get a license without a basic understanding of the laws. But sometimes drivers ignore even those and then sometimes people even die as a result. Even traffic laws can't protect everyone at all times. But that was obvious and that was not what was on his mind at all. He was thinking about something else entirely.

There exists an unwritten code amongst drivers. This code is an extension of basic human decency. Courtesy. Every driver owes it to the rest of us to remain vigilant. We all share these roads. We all pay for these roads. When we observe the rules there is order. Chaos means death at high speeds. Even at low speeds when conditions are right. Proceed through an intersection after your light turns red because your mind is elsewhere, even just for a moment, and things happen that can never be undone. Carelessness behind the wheel puts everyone at risk. What could be more selfish than endangering strangers in pursuit of making the happenings of your specific day barely more efficient?

Student drivers were a different story. Everyone deserves a chance to learn. That's why those cars are brandished with warning magnets. That's part of the code and part of the courtesy. But the asshole on the road? The guy or gal in his or her own world who loses sight of the fact that a car is a weapon when you lose respect for it? There is no excuse for that person. Those people. He could tell the difference between inexperience and carelessness just by watching drivers' behaviors. Watching their choices. He believed he had an eye for it.

He had not made it out of Corsequette yet.

Up ahead the traffic began to bottleneck. There were several lanes offering several options. All a driver needed to do was read the signs. Or read the paint on the pavement. What more could any driver require? The signage clearly spelled out what to do for every possible choice and way ahead of time. There should be no confusion unless a driver is not paying attention. He appreciated the order of it all. The planning involved. The clarity. Left to downtown. Right to the express lane. Stay in the center to bypass both. Simple directives and very clear. He stayed in the center lane and the traffic began to slow. This was as happens at times and was to be expected. This was still order and the absence of chaos. The driver of the white dually had had enough of chaos and this was not that. Sometimes traffic slows. Allow it. Allow for it. Patience. He enjoyed being on exactly the right path no matter how slow or fast he might travel upon it. The tortoise and never the hare. Eventually all vehicles stopped and waited their turns to proceed. This was order also.

The traffic began to move again and a shiny new black SUV cut directly in front of him from the right lane. No signal. No regard for the established order. This was not the move of a student. This was the learned behavior of a habitual asshole of the road.

The driver of the white dually pounded his right fist onto the horn and he kept it there. The driver of the black SUV looked back over his shoulder. The driver in the white dually studied the brief gaze for any sort of remorse. Any acknowledgment that this decision was indeed a dick move and any acknowledgement that the driver of the black SUV was owning his own behavior. That would have been at least the courteous thing to do and perhaps it would have excused the whole incident. Everyone deserves the chance to make amends if an amends can be made. But no such courtesy was extended. Instead apathy and obliviousness. Maybe even entitlement. The driver in the black SUV continued on up the lane as if he deserved to be there all along. That was the end of his consideration.

This town. This damn town. Asshole grew up right here, no doubt.

He had almost escaped Corsequette's grasp. He thought about that. He thought about everything in his truck bed and in his trailer. Both piled up with chaos and he hated chaos. He didn't have an opportunity to pack properly and he had to throw his halted life into random containers and as quickly as possible and it sickened him to treat so many separate lives that way. He thought about the previous year and the abysmal year before that. He thought about what had happened to set all of this in motion. Where was the order in any of it? He looked at the black SUV moving away and apparently speeding in the process. To his eye at least. It would not stop. It would never stop. None of it. He thought about all of it and the old noise came back.

No. He said it to himself and in perfect cadence with the noise in his skull. For once both parties inside the truck's cabin were in agreement. No. Not this time. He is part of this. He is this town and he is my landlord and he is my leasing agent and he is my temp supervisor and he might even be... No. The man in the white dually would not allow himself to finish that thought but he had already gone too far to stop himself. Something had tipped over. I've got money and I've got everything I own with me and I've got nowhere else to go and I've got all the time in the world. He will answer for it. He will answer for all of it.

Past this bit of congestion the interstate opened up again to three lanes heading north and all of them were moving along merrily enough. Saturdays are happy days and especially during the holidays. He stayed in the center lane and kept his eye on the black SUV pulling away up ahead. Maybe a quarter mile of road separated the two vehicles but they were bonded together now. Unsplitable as atomic particles inside a nucleus. Endless miles of road lie to the north. Straight and smooth and distant. No need to be anything other than patient. Clear skies and a crisp temperature and very little wind. It was a great morning for driving.

T-Bone Steak and Eggs

The man in the black SUV was traveling east from Baton Rouge. He had made the turn north onto I-55 and he was ready to settle in for a long stretch. He kept starting different playlists and he kept giving up on them after two songs at most. Nothing satisfied him at all. Where he looked to find peace he only found a deeper sense of restlessness. Endlessly fidgeting. Chewing on old drinking straws and drumming his fingers on the center armrest and shifting his weight from one asscheek to the other. So many miles ahead. So many hours. More than he could reasonably cover in one day's time.

All he wanted was something that would passively drone on in the background while his mind wandered off to wherever it needed to go. A soundtrack to help fill the void with something a bit more familiar and more comforting than the detached hiss of white noise and yet something that would not require any sort of participation on his part. This was harder to find than he would have supposed. Nothing offered that exact balance. Everything always wanted something from him. His 80s mix was too synthy and his 70s Country Gold mix was too twangy and his Hairy Metal mix was too angry and too cheesy and finally he just gave up and shut off the radio altogether. He drove on in silence and he thought about his mom. How she made great iced tea.

His mind drifted from there to the unpleasant reality that he alone would be left to settle all of his mom's affairs after she passed. There might be the sudden appearance of fringe relatives with surprising amounts of tears and grief and covetousness. These would be looking to sort through his mom's museum of useless clutter hoping to unearth anything of monetary value by which to remember our dearly departed Violet. But none of these would linger long enough to help him sort through the rest of it.

Emptying that house. The job would certainly suck whenever it became his to oversee. Maybe it was the memory of that ceramic iced tea pitcher that took him there. He could still see the crackling in the glaze from ages of faithful usage. His mom had received it from her grandmother. Or her great-grandmother or some other ancient ancestor he had never met but was expected to revere notwithstanding. A faded picture predating his birth in an old album and absent any other context. His mom loved that pitcher. It was an heirloom. He wondered if it were still in her house and he instantly knew better. Where else would it be? The old pitcher was still there all right. So was every other thing she had ever touched or had ever laid eyes on. Each of those things was an heirloom as well.

Piles of keepsakes and piles of other things had long since swallowed the entire house where he was born in Chicago. Every item was attached to a memory and every item had a story. But memories and even stories are not transferable and so the man had no use for any of it. Mom had always said she intended to sort through those piles to do God knows what with if she ever got the chance. Drove him crazy whenever she'd run out that buzz phrase as a blanket excuse. Every time she said "I just haven't had the chance to [perform any unpleasant task]" in his presence he would bite his knuckle because venting his frustration would have been disrespectful. But the resentment had been boiling for years and he really needed to get some of that old vitriol off his chest and it is a wonder he never blew up at her while she was yet up to the conflict. But he never did.

As far as he could see she had every chance to do whatever she wanted to do every day for the last twenty years and without any interference at all. Nothing but an empty agenda each day and every day. Now she was in skilled nursing and had been for two months and now she was asleep for more hours each day than she was awake and she had not so much as stood upon her own two feet for weeks. She had run out of chances to do anything at all other than lay there in that pitiful state. Each hour slipping past the more optimistic hour that preceded it. She had waited too long.

He knew all of that garage-sale clutter was still piled up inside that stuffy old tenement in Chicago where he was born. Piled up there exactly as it had been for years and years. That cat litter smell. That stale geriatric nicotine stench hanging in the rafters to which she had grown nosedeaf so many years ago. All of it would soon be his to deal with. He really would have preferred to bulldoze the whole thing but he would never do that to her. It mattered to her so soon it would have to matter to him, at least on some level. It made him feel overwhelmed and made him feel resentful and it made him kick himself to feel that way. A good son a bad son. A good son a bad son. He drove on.

That old house. It had been locked up and vacant ever since his mom had moved into assisted living. He had paid a neighbor to keep an eye on things while he and his mom were away. What did that even mean: to keep an eye on things? Someone else cut the grass and he had forwarded the mail to his own house in Louisiana. The Chicago house itself was still stationary as far as he knew. Minus a break-in, what would have pressed this neighbor on retainer into action? What was he even paying for? Probably that same elusive peace in another equally elusive form. Whatever. This line of thought was pointless and he was too fidgety already. Maybe he just needed breakfast.

He was coming up on Jackson Mississippi and he decided to stop for a bite to eat. Why not? He could get no further than St. Louis today and he had no doubt he would get that far eventually. What's an hour, plus or minus? A plywood billboard promised that a local diner was somewhere near the next exit and this was perfect. Something about diners always made him feel like a regular even if he had never seen the place before. Today was a good day to be counted amongst the locals whomever they might happen to be. And there would be fresh coffee.

The Eat Good All Day looked as if its bones had been originally erected to serve some other purpose entirely. And that ages ago. Perhaps it was once a general store and it might have been a filling station sometime after that. Somewhere post World War II it had changed hands and had been remodeled into a diner and not so much as a booth cushion had been replaced since the grill first warmed up in the late 1940s. The owner of the black SUV walked in through the vestibule and he knew at once he had made the right choice. No franchise would have it, and what higher praise exists for any restaurant?

Some red and gold and silver Christmas tinsel had been draped around the place in a reluctant and half-assed observance of the season. On the counter next to the register was a bizarrely nostalgic acrylic lighted Santa that likely warmed the hearts of all visiting senior citizens while simultaneously creeping out every unfortunate child who gazed upon its haunting and soulless countenance. Saint Nick had a nose reddened with busted capillaries likely indicating a prolonged and failing battle with high-octane booze. But he and his celebrated obesity and his jolly alcoholism certainly belonged right there next to the toothpick roller and the saucer full of green peppermints.

Several men with weathered clothes and worse faces sat at the high counter and the owner of the black SUV took the lone open stool right within their midst. That gap was usually filled by a man named Vic who apparently was at home today with the shits and nobody was supposed to sit on his stool in his absence. Had the owner of the black SUV been a local he would have understood this without being told. But he was not a local and that much was obvious. The boys on the other stools shot him a look that was not quite a warning, but the visitor was too distracted to be intimidated or even to notice any breech of local etiquette. Somehow he had come home as far as he was concerned.

A haggard woman wearing the name Freda on her lapel badge set an empty coffee cup in front of him. He told Freda that he took his coffee black and as hot as she could serve it. His stoolmates gave the slightest of nods and began to accept the temporary presence of the interloper sitting atop Vic's stool. So long as he minded his manners. Had he asked for any sort of fancypants creamer we might have an entirely different story to tell. Even small choices can sometimes account for large divergences.

Saturday mornings are typically very busy inside roadside diners like the Eat Good All Day and this was doubly true over the holidays. In addition to Vic's buddies, numerous pods of locals came into the diner especially early on these weekends hoping to stake their claims on their usual tables exactly the way church members cordon off their pews from uppity visitors on Easter Sunday. The diner's doors remaining open at all depended entirely on hungry traveling families stopping in and splurging on all sorts of elaborate breakfast combos they would never order back home, and the daily patrons with their bottomless coffee and maybe oatmeal or bran cereal didn't like them very much. With their loud talking and their coming in like they owned the place and their having no regard for how long we've lived in this town and for how long we've been coming in here and drinking this same coffee. Morning after morning after morning and kindly get the hell out.

Today there were plenty of both sorts inside the Eat Good All Day. The owner of the black SUV was in fact appreciated by management because at least he did not take up a whole table for himself alone and that meant other holiday travelers didn't have to wait as long to be seated. Lots of traveling singletons pull that move and are thus loathed among the waitstaff in obsequent silence. Another man had come in and done that very thing about ten minutes after the owner of the black SUV took his stool at the high counter. This other man wanted coffee and water only and he just sat there occupying an entire booth by himself. No one else coming. He sort of waved Freda off in a way her experience had taught her to understand meant leave me be. And so she did. He stirred his coffee vigorously and added a robust amount of sugar into its empty blackness.

The man atop Vic's stool was ready to order.

"Freda, honey. It is Freda, right? Yeah. I think I'm gonna have your T-bone steak and eggs." The stoolboys all looked at him. Big spender. Equal parts admiration and resentment. "Medium rare but extra pink. Eggs scrambled with cheese. How are the hash browns?"

"They're good."

"Right. And make em crispy. Also an English muffin and some honey. Thanks." He went back to scrolling on his phone.

Tommy was the alpha in Vic's absence. This had gone on long enough. Were they supposed to just sit here on their Saturday morning and keep silent just because an ignorant stranger had bisected their company? No. Forget all that. No one invited this guy to sit here with us and we're gonna do what we always do. By Tommy's reckoning this meant they would talk around him as if he did not exist. Let him sit there silently and eat his spendy steak and play with his fancy phone and mind his own damn business. And then he can get the hell out just like the rest of this damn bunch up in here today.

"Ronnie, you going fishing later today? Heard you talking about trying to find some crappie this weekend. Maybe Wednesday morning was it? When you mentioned it, I mean."

Tommy was all the way left and Ronnie was all the way right. Five stools in total and Vic's with the interloper was in the center. Ronnie leaned in. He might have been a bit hard of hearing. Tommy was striking up a conversation from the opposite side of the high counter with three bodies in between. Plenty of yakity yak and typical diner clatter on this holiday Saturday morning. Full house and a jukebox too. But none of those barriers were Ronnie's problem.

"Say again?"

"I say I think you was talking about crappie back on Wednesday or whatnot. You still going today?"

Tommy knew the answer to this question better than Ronnie did. It was Tommy's idea on Wednesday and it was Tommy's boat and Tommy was the one taking Ronnie fishing in the first place. The other two stoolbuddies had also been there during Wednesday's crappie discussion. Jerry was the brightest of the four. He knew what Tommy was up to.

"Well, I hope you boys pull in a bunch a slabs today. Crappie. Best meat on the water!"

All four nodded in agreement. The man atop Vic's stool nodded also. The two regulars on his left and the two regulars on his right were astounded. Who was he to listen in on their conversation? On the other hand this man drinks hot black coffee and he seems to be familiar with crappie and he even has an opinion about them. Steve could not leave it alone. Way too interesting. City folk don't know crappie.

"Excuse me, mister. I seen you nodding there. You ever catch any crappie up your way?" Steve figured the man for a yankee and Steve was right. In truth the man atop Vic's stool was an Illinois native forcibly relocated to Louisiana in his youth and that was some forty years removed. He had lived in Baton Rouge since he was nine years old and he could make an excellent crawdad gumbo.

Good for him! Those notable facts piled all together changed nothing at all. He was a yankee alright.

"Sure! Sure. My granddad used to take me all the time when I was a kid. Had him a brush pile." They all nodded again.

"Brush pile," said Ronnie into his coffee cup. "Can't beat a good brush pile."

"No sir." He said sir and their opinion of the man continued its uptick. "Some days we'd go there and nothing. You know. Then again." He sipped his coffee. "Sometimes we'd get a bucket a minnows and it was like every fish in lake liked to jump right in the boat with us! Had to duck! I swear sometimes we'd run outta bait and they'd still be fighting over them empty gold hooks!"

"Ha!" said Jerry. "I need me one a them brush piles!"

All laughed. He wasn't Vic but he would do for today. They went around the horn exchanging granddad fishing stories and every stoolboy had one. Even Tommy. Then the steak showed up and they talked about the best ways to grill a good piece of meat. Assuming Johnny on the grill was out of earshot, the four locals explained that they never order the T-bone at the Eat Good All Day because they don't know how to cook a decent steak and besides the cut was cheap and full of gristle. Vic's substitute said it was fine for what it was: something to eat with scrambled eggs and hash browns. They gave Johnny on the grill that much at credit at least. Reluctantly. Priced kinda high though. But have you seen the cost of steak these days? Mercy.

The steak was gone and the man owning the black SUV realized he had been sitting there long enough. He remembered the long drive yet ahead of him and he remembered he still had work to do on that bluetooth thing and he knew he wasn't getting any closer to finishing either unpleasant task by chewing the fat over granddad brush piles with Mississippi locals. He dismounted Vic's stool and dispensed nods all around.

"Well, thank you boys. I better git."

"Alright." said Steve. "Good luck with your momma." Granddad talk eventually turned into what-brings-you-up-this-way talk and the man had told them. They respected any son going to help his momma in her time of need. Even mommas way up in Chicago.

"Thanks. It's tough alright. Miss Freda, I'm ready for my check."

"Oh, you don't have a check, honey. Man over yonder paid fer your breakfast."

"Really? What man? I don't know anyone in here today."

Freda looked around. The elongated booth was empty.

"That's funny. I guess he left. He didn't even order anything to eat. Just sat there and maybe drank one cup a coffee. If that. Hm. Well. Isn't that something! Sometimes people just do nice things this time a year. Never know when you're entertaining angels, do ya? Have a nice day now and drive safe. And Merry Christmas!"

Picking Up the Check

Black SUVs on the interstate are ubiquitous. They are also ubiquitous on every other sort of road and in every parking lot and in any other place where vehicles tend to congregate. Even their owners often exit grocery stores and approach convincing clones and become angry and agitated when their fancy key fobs refuse to help them empty their overfilled shopping carts into the wrong vehicles. Where's the beeping? Lights flashing? Where's that automatic hatch-open when you actually need the thing to assist you? It certainly opens every time you need your hatch to stay closed. Walk at a typical pace around the rear to the driver's side and up flies the damn hatch every time. Except when you insist on unloading your groceries into someone else's black SUV. All those fobs can manage in such instances is to make some distant horn chirp away from underneath the hood of some random car outside of the equation and also two rows over. That's assuming the owner got close enough to trigger any response at all. How is this helpful? How is this better? And somehow those useless fobs cost hundreds of dollars to replace when broken or lost.

So many black SUVs on the road. Every make must have one. How was the man in the white dually going to keep from losing his prey while following this obvious asshole of the road at an inconspicuous distance when said asshole is driving the most duplicated vehicle possible? Lane changes and speed traps and last-minute exits and also road hazards. Look away for a moment and you might end up following a doppelgänger down an onramp to a rest stop and only then discover the sleight of hand that ruined your day. Then you'd have to choose between exacting vengeance on an innocent or else giving up entirely. A bad choice and not one easily made. He couldn't allow himself to be put in that position. Luckily this particular asshole had made following the trail a lot easier for the man in the white dually. Of course he had.

The rear windshield of the black SUV in question was adorned with an oversized gold New Orleans football helmet decal across the center and also a bass fishing sticker in the lower right corner. The bass sticker likely meant the driver enjoyed fishing and the two men might have bonded over that under different circumstances. But that would never do now. Never mind. At the very least the driver of the white dually was certain that big helmet decal interfered with the black SUV driver's rearview line of sight and this came as no surprise to him at all. Selfishness is a learned behavior. Far more important for all passing motorists to understand the asshole's rooting interests than it was for him to work around his blind spots while changing lanes. And announcing that he was likely a fisherman as well was certainly information the rest of the world needed. The absolute narcissism involved in putting such things on cars. Why do people do things like this? Just drive; who cares what you like or don't like? The man in the white dually shook his head and the conceit on display solidified his hatred by a few additional degrees. He knew this man. His type at least. The picture was already clear and becoming clearer.

Of course a guy who just forces his way into someone else's lane and expects others to adjust themselves to his intrusion also covers his vehicle in irrelevant personal fetishes at the further expense of general safety. It is on the rest of us to watch out for him. Make allowances for him. This football fan and bass fisherman has implicit right of way. Yield to him. Yield to him in all things and at all times. He is more important than you. A guy like this has never thought of anyone but himself. He is in it to win it. What does that mean: in it to win it? To take from others what should belong to them? To assume you are the favored? To put yourself first in all situations? Every encounter a zero-sum game and always your advantage to the detriment of every other player? No deference. No grace for others. No forgiveness. Yeah. He knew him alright. He hated people who struggled with forgiveness. We all need grace sometimes.

The black SUV with the New Orleans helmet sticker and the fishing sticker was signaling an intention to exit. Its driver was using a turn indicator. For a moment the man in the white dually was taken aback. He had put it past the man in the black SUV to observe such a courteous practice and especially in this situation. No other cars were particularly close to the black SUV. The cogs of his loathing slipped a few clicks of traction but quickly recovered whatever ground was lost. Sure. He'll signal when it is convenient for him to do so. He is probably congratulating himself for obeying the law. The smugness of it. He hated him more.

The road was paved across a series of gentle hills and when the black SUV diverted to the offramp the man in the white dually lost sight of him momentarily. Bit of panic. But the black SUV again became visible on the distant upslope and so the man reassured himself that the day yet remained unruined. He exited the interstate and continued his pursuit.

Perhaps the black SUV needed fuel or its driver might have needed a restroom break but the driver of the white dually doubted either case. Those were needs. This was probably a selfish move like all his other selfish moves. When he saw the black SUV pull into the parking lot of the Eat Good All Day, the man in the white dually felt vindicated. Of course. Gotta stop and stuff your face. You're probably in for a long road trip or even a short road trip and you have plenty of money to burn. Dontcha? Can't go through a drive thru and grab a simple combo meal or God forbid you put yourself out and pack some modest sandwiches ahead of time to eat along the way. Especially since we already know that driving while distracted doesn't bother you at all. Wouldn't even be a problem.

But oh no. No small cooler for you. You're the type who needs to indulge all his appetites to the fullest and whenever they arise. Gotta pick the biggest item on the menu and eat till your belly bursts. Dontcha? He pulled the white dually into a space at the back of the lot and let the engine idle. This will tell us all I need to know, I bet.

The man in the white dually opened his glove box and took out his snubnose .357 and he opened the wheel. There were four bullets already loaded. He took out the open box of shells and he placed two additional rounds in the empty chambers. Fully loaded now. He flipped the wheel shut and held in in his hand. Felt the weight of it. He knew what fully loaded felt like. His thoughts drifted back to his wife and his little girl and suddenly his agenda became very different. Why was he here? God, he missed them so much. He put his head on the steering wheel. He held the gun across his chest and he called their names and the tears began flowing like new streams along an ancient and angry creek bed. The parched and pancake-cracked flesh of his weathered cheeks was beginning to soften. He looked at his .357 and he imagined that it could transport him to wherever they were right now. This mental exercise was a bad road and he still understood that much. He tried to catch his breath and sort out all the different feelings currently fighting for control over his mind and over his soul. No, he said. They would be disappointed, he said. Stuff to do yet.

He looked up and into the rearview and saw the truck bed and the trailer with all of his belongings covered under blue tarps and he sobbed some more. It was difficult to sort out why exactly. He wasn't sad to leave Louisiana. That certainly wasn't it. Maybe he was sad to learn that several entire lives could be so easily packaged and quantified. Was this all there was? He looked back down at his piece and threw it into the passenger seat beside him. Focus, he said.

He remembered his current mission and suddenly it didn't make a lot of sense. He wiped his cheeks. For a solid minute he forgot why he hated the man in the black SUV and he nearly gave up the idea entirely. He sat there and fixed his eyes forward and tried to orient his thoughts. Why was he here? Why specifically? What had led him to this? In the closest possible parking space to the front door other than those allocated to the handicapped was a black SUV with a gold New Orleans helmet decal plastered across the center of the rear windshield and also a bass fishing sticker in the lower right corner. That old noise saw its chance to pin the man's chin against his skull and then it gave his old pain a nudge to step to the plate and swing for the fences. You're up, it said.

Teeth clenched and grinding away their irreplaceable enamel. The bottomless pain in his soul and no one left alive to blame for it. He'd do, this man driving his sparkly new black SUV and clearly an asshole of the road. Brand new and you couldn't wait to sticker it all up and make it ugly. Did you manage to park close enough? Wouldn't want you to take any unnecessary steps and burn an extra calorie or two walking your fat ass across a parking lot. Wouldya?

He looked at the .357 lying loaded and full and upturned in the passenger seat. No, he said. There will be families in there. I have all the time in the world and this asshole will make a mistake and I'll be there when he does. He picked up the pistol and returned it to its holster inside the glovebox. He closed the lid. Let's go in and see what we can see. The man shut off the engine and applied the parking brake. He stepped outside the truck and walked inside the diner.

When the owner of the white dually entered the Eat Good All Day he was uncertain as to how to identify his new enemy. The fact had not occurred to him before that moment. The memory of his face in the rearview during that brief encounter was fuzzy and fading and now the owner of the black SUV could be any man inside the diner this morning. Back to Square One. But then he remembered that was not true. The owner of the black SUV was selfish and also an asshole. He would be easy enough to spot in a room full of normal people. Just have to pay attention. A snake cannot change its spots.

A hostess attempted to seat the man at the low counter and he refused. There was no way to survey the entire floor from that vantage point. He instead pointed to a solitary booth at the back center of the dining hall and the hostess was reluctant. It could accommodate as many as a party of six holiday traveling guests and this man was all by himself. After a brief exchange she remembered that she was paid minimum wage and this man was insistent approaching hostile and any tip he might leave or any hypothetical traveling party of six might have left instead would not be split with her in either event so she was not about to argue with him. Fine. Booth for six for one. The man thanked her.

A waitress with the name Freda embossed on a plastic badge came over and was instantly irritated that one of the choice booths in her section was now occupied by a singleton guest and on a Saturday over the holidays. She asked him what he wanted to drink and he told her he wanted coffee and water and that he did not need a menu. Dammit. She knew it and it was even worse than she thought. Not even gonna order any food. She brought him a cup and a handful of creamers. These he flicked to the side. He grabbed the sugar and poured too much of it into the cup. He stirred aimlessly and without ceasing, the spoon clanking rhythmically.

From his elongated booth he scanned the room. He was pretty sure this guy was also alone although he wasn't sure how he knew this. But it was an important detail now. Any tables and booths with families or even couples were summarily ruled out. That cut the possibilities down to less than a quarter of the patrons inside. Good sleuthing, he thought. What remained were three tables and the two sets of barstools. Two of the tables occupied by solitary guests were women. One was older and one was younger but these distinctions didn't matter. He had seen his nemesis well enough to know he was a man. Of course he was a man! He would never consider pursuing this vendetta had it been a woman who cut him off on I-55. He had been raised too well for all that. This was a man-to-man problem and it would be handled man to man. Assuming his asshole counterpart was up to the challenge.

He hoped the owner of the black SUV also carried a pistol and he imagined them squaring off for a duel behind the Eat Good All Day somewhere between the dumpsters and the loading dock. There would be dignity in that. Time honored. Order and not chaos. And honestly any outcome would have been a welcomed end to it all. The end to this battle and to the end of the long con that had been his entire life up to and including this very morning. But he knew he wasn't that lucky. At least he had not been that lucky for the last two years and for a lengthy stretch before that. No way this guy carried a handgun. More likely he voted to prevent others from doing so. Stripping law abiding citizens of their constitutional rights to protect themselves from criminals and from the otherwise obviously guilty. Oh, how he hated this man.

One solitary guest was a man that appeared to be too old for serious consideration. He felt sorry for the old man. Eating a poached egg and some dry toast by himself and mumbling away perhaps to provide himself a substitute for sentient company. Where were his people? His family? This was Christmastime after all. That line of questioning began veering too close to the sun and he abandoned it just in time. Who else was in here?

The low counter or the high counter? Hmm. The low counter comprised six stools in total and three of them were occupied. There was a twosome and a singleton. The singleton was a man in post office garb and this all but disqualified him instantly. In the first place it is hard work being a mailman. The sort of person he was tracking was naturally repulsed by hard work so that was Strike One. Secondly this postman appeared to be keeping to himself and such behavior simply did not track at all. The sort of man currently disgusting the owner of the white dually would likely go through life assuming he was starring in his own movie. The rest of the world were merely extras or at best the supporting cast. As such their lives would be made infinitely more interesting were he but to acknowledge their replaceable existences with any splash of attention whatsoever. This sort of man would naturally fill any vacuum of peaceful silence with personal answers to questions no one in the diner was asking. Maybe some postmen would do this also but not this postman. All he appeared to want was breakfast. Good man. On to the high counter. And there he was.

It was him. It had to be him. Of course it was him. All the owner of the white dually had to do was look at center stage of the high counter and there he found his asshole of the road. He clinched his fist without being aware of it. The pairs on either side of the centerpiece were of one sort and the man in the middle was clearly of another. That checked out. He was fat of the belly and that naturally made sense as well. Gluttonous and lazy. And this man at Stool 3 seemed to have no idea that he was an intruder amongst a foursome who certainly belonged there. From the elongated booth meant for six people occupied by himself alone, the owner of the white dually recognized the hallmarks of unbridled entitlement. The asshole was everything he thought him to be. Selfishness personified. Animated and in the flesh.

He thought about going out to get his .357 and he began to wonder who in the Eat Good All Day would blame him if he shot the owner of the black SUV right there at the high counter. And he wondered who would dare to testify against him. More likely they would pick up his tab and provide him with an alibi on his way heading further north. Maybe it could happen right here. No, he said. Calm down, he said. You came in here to learn.

Freda came by to heat up his coffee but there was no room to even top off the cup. He did not look at her and yet still waved her off with his left hand. Jerk. Absolute jerk. She understood all right and she committed herself to never returning to his booth should hell itself freeze over while his unfriendly ass sat there waiting on hotter coffee. And she'd tell him so herself if only he had the sac to complain within earshot. Freda has her own story and she was at the end of her own rope today but no one in the Eat Good All Day took notice. Least of all the owner of the white dually.

With no further interruptions he leaned in across the table and listened. This was not easy. Two full rows of tables lay between his elongated booth and the high counter but he managed to piece together a few things.

There was talk of a mother in Chicago. He implied he was taking care of her in some way and that this trip was a duty of sorts to her. This new information was in every way inconvenient to the leech profile the owner of the white dually had constructed for the owner of the black SUV. He'd sort that out later. This guy probably just wanted a fat inheritance or something. No doubt he was exaggerating the nature of this supposed selfless act. Maybe he wanted all her stuff. No doubt he was ready to sell off her lifetime for pennies on the dollar. That was probably it.

Gotta be a golfer, this guy. He hated golfers.

There was talk of being newly landed in the South and this did track with his profile perfectly but there was also talk of crappie fishing. He doubted this man had ever seen a crappie in his whole damn life. Maybe he had read about them in one of those airline promo mags they stick inside the seatbacks in front of you when you fly. Maps with boastful travel routes and ads for steakhouses conveniently located in hub cities and other fluff intended to reinforce their dominance in the air travel industry, as if an abundance of choices were still available. And there was no doubt this guy traveled plenty. That much was certain. Bet he had enough rewards miles to stay at a 5-star casino on the lunar surface this Christmas Eve. Probably pissed his sick momma ruined his trip, the louse. Then his order came.

With great relief the man owning the white dually learned that the man owning the black SUV had ordered T-bone steak and eggs. The world made sense again. Of course this asshole of the road could not satisfy himself with a simple combination of eggs and bacon and toast or maybe a breakfast sandwich. He had to throw in for the biggest-ticket item on the menu. The white dually owner let out a sigh of relief and embraced his hatred in full bloom and reckoned it fully justified. There he was in the midst of blue-collar regulars and he had to put on airs by buying T-bone steak for breakfast. That would make the locals notice him and hate him. And he was half right which is the same as being completely wrong.

The man owning the white dually strained his ears hoping to hear the regulars take their separate turns at the gall on display and he was astounded by what he heard but in utterly the wrong way. Yes this black SUV owner was conversing with the local regulars as if he belonged there and yes he was talking about crappie fishing as if he knew the first thing about it and yes he freely admitted a birth in Chicago of all places. But no. Somehow they did not hate him for any of those horrible things.

In fact he appeared to be duping them! And boy! Could this guy slather on the good ol' boy vernacular to please his audience! Dropping Gs like an authentic hick from Any Southern State USA. They actually bought his sacrificial story concerning his intent to help his poor sick momma up in Chicagoland. Bet she wasn't sick at all. If there even was a momma up there. But even worse: after listening to all his horseshit they all became absolutely chummy! Started talking about the best ways to cook steak on a grill of all things and they acted like the owner of the black SUV might actually have something useful to contribute to the conversation! Could they not smell the douchebag reeking off of him? Damn! The man owning the white dually could barely choke down two swallows of his sweet coffee for the stench of it in his nostrils and here they were inhaling clouds of it by the lungful and inviting him to spew forth even more of it. He was embarrassed for the locals. Trucker caps and work shirts and boots and chew rings and none of that stood a chance against his white-collar smarmy mojo. A damned disgrace is what it was.

These local rubes might have fallen for the charade but not the owner of the white dually. He was not fooled and would never be fooled. Pursuing this man would be his new life until whenever his permanent new life showed itself. Freda circled back on her way to a paying table and he softly grabbed her by the left forearm.

"Excuse me, ma'am," he said. "That handsome fatty gentleman at the high counter. Right there in the middle? White headed and candyassed. You see him, dontcha? Looks like he never worked a day in his life?"

"What can I do for you, sir?" She was still annoyed to have a singleton in her elongated booth and one only drinking coffee. Freda really needed money and she needed it today. It never occurred to the man that she might have an opinion about him one way or the other.

"I'm about to leave. But whatever cash I put down here is meant to cover my coffee and water and your tip for both tickets and his big ol T-bone breakfast. Hear me? He don't pay a dime of what he owes. We'll settle up later, him and me."

"Oh, that's nice, mister. Who should I say bought him his breakfast?"

"Oh, he don't know me. Not yet. Don't worry about that, darling. I'll introduce myself to him in due time. Thank you kindly."

"My goodness! We don't often see that sort of kindness in here. Most people are mostly just worried about themselves these days. Are you a Christian?"

The question bothered him and it bothered him a lot. He certainly thought he was a Christian but even grunting a noise towards the affirmative was suddenly a bone in the throat.

"What do you mean, ma'am?"

"Nothing. I was just assuming you thought yous doing your Christian duty is all."

"Uh huh. I guess I am. If you read the right parts of the Good Book, I mean. Lots a stuff is in there. You just have to know where to look for what you need and then ya just sorta ignore the other parts that might get in your way. Know what I mean?"

"No, not really. But have a nice day anyway and God bless you! You done a real nice thing. Made my day, mister. Merry Christmas!"

In the presence of such a thoughtful gesture Freda abandoned all of her former animosity towards the owner of the white dually. The holidays were a kind and forgiving time after all. Freda left the elongated booth occupied by a singleton and continued on her route to the coffee urn. She grabbed a fresh pot off the forward burner and she continued moving at a steady clip, serving her traveling customers with newly found inspiration and vigor that would last for the better part of an hour.

The man owning the white dually looked at the center stool at the high counter with renewed disgust. Chicago. He had believed enough of the overheard horseshit to accept that this trip might indeed take him all the way up there. Never been anywhere near there before. Never seen any of the Great Lakes. Why not? I'll follow you to Juneau if that's what it takes to have my peace, mister. Drive. I'm on your six.

He peeled off two twenty-dollar bills from a roll in his pocket and dropped them onto the formica table and he headed out through the vestibule and back to the parking lot. Only two sips gone from his coffee and he didn't even need those. Caffeine was useless today.

He started his engine and he waited. The other man took an additional twelve minutes to return to his black SUV. Another minute later and he was back on the access road looking to merge onto I-55 North once again. The man in the white dually put his truck in gear and resumed following the black SUV at a casual pace. It was a productive stop. At least he understood the game now.

The First of Three Unpleasant Phone Calls

He had just finished his breakfast and the day was still newish and yet he couldn't put it off any longer. Four missed calls already. That ringtone belonged to Scott, his direct supervisor. A sales guru of sorts who had been in the industrial copier leasing industry for eleven years fewer than the driver of the black SUV. They had worked together in this company for three years before the guru's promotion. Scott was also much younger than the man driving up north to see his dying mother. When the driver himself had been a young up-and-comer in the industry he never understood why his age was apparently such an issue for so many older colleagues. He understood now.

He knew Scott was really good at closing deals but he used all the wrong angles in doing so. Over promise. Under deliver. Extend. Vagueness. Fuzzy quotes. Douchey smarmy oily charm intended as a substitute for genuine charisma. He expected the same from his direct reports including the man driving the black SUV but he just couldn't make himself do it. Didn't know how. But this was the order of things and he tried to be pragmatic about becoming obsolete. The new always eat the old and so be it. This was natural and he knew it was time for him to step away and let new ideas have their say. But the man hadn't quite left yet. This meant that for now he had to continue dealing with Scott Shetland and Scott was calling him already.

Pragmatism aside, it was still so hard to take Scott Shetland seriously. The driver of the black SUV had picked up on the fact that Scott often used incorrect words in conversation. They sounded similar to the words he intended to use but they were the wrong words and they did not quite mean the same things. He could still be understood but this idiosyncrasy occurred often enough to be distracting to the careful listener. A thing impossible to ignore once detected. Every time his boss inserted an awkward substitution the man felt a flinch in his soul. Metaphysical and grammatical arrhythmia. He also often mispronounced slightly tricky words and God help him and God help us all.

That ringtone again.

Now I guess. A holiday Saturday and he was at work just yesterday and already Scott was calling. Did the man ever sleep? This level of persistence was surprising even for his douchey boss but a call like this was coming eventually so right now was as good a time as any. Fine, you bastard. Let's do it.

He fumbled with his dashboard media controls and he managed to answer the call through some sort of fancy onboard interface. Made him a bit proud of himself in some vague and self-patronizing way. Good for me. Look! Even I can do this. What strange new doors this new vehicle was throwing open.

"Scott! Hey. How are you?"

"I'm killin it! Listen, Buddy!" The driver was not entirely sure his boss knew his real name. Or anyone else's real name. Could have been an honest mistake repeated infinitely. Maybe Scott actually believed his entire salesforce was employed solely by people named Buddy or Guy or perhaps people named Buddy and Guy at the same time. Why not? One name is as good as another. "How's it going, Guy? How's your dad?"

"Yeah, not good. He died in 2001. Lung cancer."

"Dang, Guy. Sorry to hear that. Didn't make it down there in time, I guess. Sucks. Did you get our flowers? Take all the time you need. So you'll be heading back soon, I guess?"

"Well, no. Not really. I mean, I just left maybe four hours ago and I still have about 700 miles to go before I get there. I'm actually traveling up to see my mom right now. Chicago. She's the one not doing well. Not at all. They don't expect her to improve."

"Pretty sure you told me you were going to see your dad, Buddy."

"No, no. I said my mom. My dad has been dead for nineteen years now and I would have remembered that. It's mom this time."

"Damn. Sucks, bro. Look. I hate to be that guy, Buddy. But your clients, Guy. They're blowing up my phone. Saying you're not returning their calls. I know I've installed in all my sales reps a certain core of ethics. Irregardless of our own issues, Guy, our clients come first, amiright? I know losing both your parents at once has to really blow majorly, but you're an extender of me. That means whatever you do is a reflector on me also. Hear what I'm saying?"

"I'm trying to."

"You can't lose sight of what's important. No matter how fustrating it is. I mean, we're all pulling for your parents to pull through and all. Joanie's getting a card together. You like butt cake, right? Red velvet? Sure. But I guess I'm wondering when you plan to come back, Buddy? Or at least when you're planning on making some phone calls."

"Well, Scott. It's Saturday morning and I was at work just yesterday. I have plenty of days saved up. I'm surprised you've heard from any of my clients already. On an early Saturday morning? That would be unusual even for the needy ones."

"Needy feeds the greedy. See what I did there?"

"I cleared out my service queue just yesterday. There's no way my customers have been bugging you or anyone else already this morning. Most of my clients don't work on weekends at all, Scott. And in December least of all. Where's the fire? You called me five times already."

"Wow. Sensing some hostility, Guy. This is not your A-Typical baseline. Don't get smart. Okay, Buddy. Not the enemy here. I knew you had a buttload of issues and all but I had to hear through the grape lines that you suddenly decided to up and leave town. Needed an update, Guy, so I can leverage your absence into a Plus instead of a Delta. You feel me, brotha? And I didn't say your clients specifically, Guy. I told everyone at our last SIZZLE meeting that we work together as a team. There's no I in... Remember? You were there. You get it. We're running behind as a team so we all have to up our game. Dig a little deeper. Finish the year with a synergistic critical mass that cannot be contained or even squished a little bit, Buddy. You know what I mean. Done this work forever, right? You know teamwork is indisposible."

"Scott, slow down. Please. Hear me. I told you more than a week ago that my mom had taken a turn and that I'd need to be taking some time away. But now I'm really confused. What are you saying, Scott? You want me to call people who aren't my clients? On Saturday night or on Sunday? While I'm going up to see my dying mom in Chicago?"

"That'd be solid, Buddy! But I was really trying to gouge when you thought we'd see you back in the office. Yesterday kinda threw me for a loaf, Guy. Sounded like we wouldn't be seeing you on Monday or Tuesday or who knows even."

"Scott, my mom is not going to get any better. This is her time. And I have to tend to her passing and then settle her affairs after that. Whenever that happens. I have somewhere in the neighborhood of forty days saved and I don't know how long I'll be gone. But you should expect me to be in Chicago for at least two weeks. Who knows? Might even be up there way past the new year, Scott."

"Cool. Yeah. Okay. Sure! But our office is in Baton Rouge. Not in Chicago."

"Exactly correct. I won't be in Baton Rouge for two weeks at least. Not at all. For two weeks. At least. Maybe longer. Because I'll be in Chicago instead. And I'll be honest, Scott. I had planned on making calls today and even tonight in my motel in St. Louis."

"St. Louis? Buddy. I know you just told me you were going to Chicago. Now you're going to St. Louis? First your dad, then both your parents, now just your mom? You're sort of tripping yourself up here, Guy. Get your story straight, Guy. At least try to say things that are at least simular."

"Sigh. I was planning on touching base with all of my clients to let them know I was away on family business but also to assure them that they could reach me if they really needed to. But now I don't think I'm going to do that. Whatever copier needs they have over the holidays can be better served by whomever is in the office than they could be by me up in Illinois. Besides, it's not their business and I have covered for other reps many times. That's why I still have forty days of PTO. I never use it. So I don't have a clear estimation for you on when I'll return. But you won't be hearing from me again for at least two weeks. At which point I will call you and let you know if I need to take off more time after that."

"More time? More. More than two weeks, you mean? Guy. I don't know what to say. Umm. Damn, bro. I've tried to be supportive. Pretty sure you can't do this. Just up and leave? Look. I get it. I've bailed too when I needed to get away for a while. Copiers get to your head after a while, Buddy. Been there. It's the toner. Gets into your skin and plays hell with your Zen, bro. I wish you would have just said that. Instead I gotta catch you in all these lies. Mom. Dad. St. Louis. Miami. Car trouble. Chicago. It's embarrassing. I could care less. Just tell me Jamaica, mon. Right? A little rum a little ganja and maybe even find a local hottie. Amiright? I feel ya. But you gotta put in for trips like that ahead a time. Get them on the calendar and get them cleared. You just told me yesterday and that's not cool for anybody, bro. You can't just leave for two weeks and still keep your job. If I gotta go there. I don't want to be that guy, Guy. And this team is going places, Buddy. We're flying high and I'd hate for you to miss the boat."

"Actually, I can do this. I've put in for FMLA with HR. Family illness. My job is protected. I really am tending to my mom like I said. That's where my focus needs to be right now. But I'll be back."

"I'm gonna check on that, Guy. No offense. Dang. I really didn't think this was where we were heading. I thought you were gonna tell me you'd make a few calls, no big deal, do whatever you had to do and we'd see you by Tuesday or Wednesday. You sure this is how you wanna roll, Buddy? Your move."

"Goodbye, Scott. I'll call in two weeks. And if I don't then have a Merry Christmas."

The man hit the red Disconnect button on his touchscreen and one of his playlists resumed blaring out vintage tunes both familiar and forgettable and the voice of Scott Shetland was absent entirely. Perhaps some of these overly financed features barnacled atop his intended payments were not completely useless after all.

Scott's ringtone sounded off again several times over the next two hundred miles. But eventually that ringtone stopped. There would be awkwardness later but he had been through that before. His clients liked him so he knew he'd be fine. The important development to come from all of this was that one ugly call was over with. Good but not great. There were still other calls yet to make. He kept driving and he kept stalling. He changed his playlist again and moved from the left asscheek to the right asscheek.

From Assisted Living to Skilled Nursing

His father had died in that house. He was a baker by trade and that industry was difficult at the best of times. If there ever had been a golden age of bakeries, the tenure of his father's career had clearly existed outside of it. Over the span of his entire childhood he could not remember a time when the family was caught up on bills. A shotgun house with a head start on full collapse when they bought it. Crumbling brick and a sagging front porch decimated by dry rot and decades of indifference.

Never more than one car in the driveway. Where would we put another car? This was his father's default response whenever his mother complained about needing transportation during the day. Their lot had a single-lane gravel driveway leading up to a carport designed for a single car. Parking on the street was always a sketchy proposition and so his father was not incorrect. But his dad's valid point was merely convenient and was in no way germane to the issue. His mom knew both of these truths. So did the boy and very early.

Dad smoked and drank without ceasing. He was not a mean drunk and somehow his son was grateful for this. His own appreciation for the fact bothered him at times. Why should we celebrate a man because he retains enough ingrained class to keep himself from harming his family even in the absence of inhibitions? What sort of accomplishment was this? Every evening ended in full stupor. Still. He had friends who would have traded places with him and that was awful and remarkable. In the end it was the cigarettes that took him and not the drink. Unfiltered, of course.

His generation smoked everywhere they went. Even the doctors offered smokes to their patients and the waiting rooms aways hung with stale smoke and it was all routine. Until people started dying and then there were lawsuits and warning labels and all sorts of retroactive condemnation. But the damage was already done. His father was too late in quitting. A spot on the lung and then a fast acceleration and suddenly mom was all alone. That was nineteen years ago.

She had done pretty well for herself, the stubborn old broad. He had no siblings so her care fell to himself alone. To the extent that she would allow his intrusion. How many times had he wanted her to go into an assisted living community? Mom, he said. You could have new friends and new things to do. Never have to worry about balancing your checkbook or paying your bills and the activities director will make sure you never get bored. Rest for once. Why not hear them out? But she wasn't having it. You just want to ship me off and forget all about me, she said. Sure. That would make things easier for you. Just like you left for Louisiana when things got hard and don't think I forgot that. But she did forget.

He never wanted to leave. Dad's job was hard. The boy knew that. Even though dad had a relationship with whiskey, he always went to work and even after he got sick. He punched his clock every day and took overtime when there was any. But the bakery struggled and no one running the machines on the floor had gotten a raise in three years. Inflation didn't care.

At some point the boy's mom placed a call to her mom in Louisiana and a plan began to take shape. His father hated it and cursed about it and said it was never gonna happen on his watch but ultimately he could not argue against the sense it made.

They decided to ship him off to live with her parents in Baton Rouge and maybe they could see him during summer vacations or during holidays like this one. Just until things picked up a little. His mom could find a job now. One she could walk to or one near a bus stop. The boy cried. He begged them to let him stay but the tears of a child often change nothing at all. Off he went.

His grandparents loved him and he loved living with them. Such great people and such a great way to grow into adulthood. His granddad was a huge college football fan and the boy attended many football games over the remainder of his childhood. They also had family in Shreveport and every December his granddad took him to a bowl game there no matter who was playing. The man driving the black SUV thought about that and realized that game would happen about a week from now. He wished he and his own son had tickets but then he remembered he couldn't go right now even if they did have them. Back in the day his own granddad would let him choose which team to root for and his decision was always based on mascots or on uniform colorations. They'd sit in that team's end zone and pretend to be alumni. God, that was a great time.

His granddad also taught him how to fish. Bass fishing was the big dance of course. The boy and his friends could tend to that in their fancy bass boats with their monster 75-horse outboards and seeing-eye sonar gadgets. They could have all that mess. But crappie fishing was where the boy and his granddad really bonded. He had a secret brush pile where crappie stacked up like cord wood. A galvanized johnboat and a 15-horse motor. Bucket of minnows and orange and yellow bobbers and soon enough supper was on the table. He hated cleaning those fish but eventually the chore became rote and meaningless. Just a thing you did to eat a good supper. And he loved gumbo too. The making of it especially. But none of this was a substitute for growing up with his parents and he tried not to become resentful. But Mom didn't make it easy.

Add together the passing decades and the dementia and the deferred regret and the anger by proxy and now the woman had somehow told herself that her son had wanted to leave them high and dry the whole time and it was even his idea in the first place.

And she resented him for being gone all those years. When her mind bent that way, which was not all the time.

Somewhere along the way the boy had become a man and he understood what was happening to his mom's brain. It was sad and she could not help it and none of that made her words any easier to endure. When she would again attempt to extract her pound of flesh for his cowardly absence, the man would kiss his mom on her forehead and wait for her mind to track elsewhere. It always did. He would hold her hand until she was again glad to see him. Again proud of him. Truth was in the tapestry somewhere tangled amongst so many threads of confusion. Sometimes she called him Roger but that was not his name.

Eventually it became clear that living alone was tantamount to elderly abuse and the man had to move his mom to a facility against her wishes. It got just as ugly as it sounds. But eventually she did begin to enjoy some new things in spite of herself. A woman there named Joy became her new best friend. They played Chicken Foot with a cheap set of dominos. Then Mom had taken a fall and had broken her hip and soon the assisted living facility was overmatched by her personal care needs. They transferred her to skilled nursing and within a month his mom had begun sliding downhill and her descent never slowed. In fact it was now accelerating and he now found himself driving up to Pleasant Latter Days under immense pressure to arrive as soon as possible.

Failure to thrive, they called it. Damn. What a dark descriptor. He understood the sentiment at least. When was the last time he remembered feeling like he was thriving? But unlike his own, her failure to thrive was brought on by a broken-down body overly tired from too many fights along the way. It was only a matter of time for her now. As if anything else were ever true for her or for him or for anyone who ever lived on planet Earth. He thought about all of this as he drove north on I-55 in his new black SUV.

He hated the baking industry and he hated unfiltered cigarettes and he hated dementia. And he decided to learn how to play Chicken Foot whenever he got back home. The internet could probably teach him.

His mom had wanted to die in that house like her husband had nineteen years before. The driver of the black SUV was burdened by a prickling criticism that maybe a good son would oblige his mom's final wishes no matter how meaningless they seemed to anyone else. This overly late concession would be a token gesture because she was past caring where her final hours might be spent but how did that change anything? He knew she wanted this when she still had some sort of say regarding her own affairs. Perhaps this was the last thing he could do for her while she yet lived. A good son a bad son. That was assuming he could make it to Chicago in time and this was anything but certain. But if she held on maybe he could force a last-minute transport back to the house. Whether the initiative was for her benefit or for his was now irrelevant. Maybe he could still make it happen and maybe it would matter somehow.

The staff at Pleasant Latter Days said her time was running short and he was still so far away. Ahead of him was St. Louis and a very short night and then up and gone before the sun ever knew he had stopped. He had made reservations at a Tremendous 10 motel with deluxe accommodations including two queens and a minifridge. Why did he bother? No time for anything other than a catnap now. But in Baton Rouge he had put his own comfort into his considerations for the journey and now all of it seemed so selfish and also stupid. Sigh. Probably shouldn't have stayed so long in Memphis but the barbecue had led him astray. Ribs. Sigh. Always his own stomach first. A good son a bad son.

A notification on his dashboard informed him that his new black SUV would need an oil change in 29 days.

Another Meal and Further Reconnaissance

The man in the black SUV exited I-55 when he came to the outskirts of Memphis. Of course he did. By now he needed to refuel and also a restroom but both of these pursuits were again secondary motives. They had to be. The man in the white dually had noticed several loud billboards for some place calling itself Nessy's Barbecue Barn and he knew the man he was following at a distance would not resist. It was just too him. Flashy. Gluttonous. Obvious. Touristy. Nessy's Barbecue Barn might have been erected with only this black SUV driver in mind. Perhaps it existed for no other purpose and would vanish forever once the men continued north. The Exit Now! billboard even mentioned that Nessy's Barbecue Barn also sold gas at an inflated price and so any remaining guesswork ended right there. The white dually began drifting towards the right lane before the black SUV did the same, even though it was some 300 yards behind the vehicle it followed.

The man in the white dually began to worry about his ability to remain hidden. If only they could reverse vehicles. Who notices another random black SUV in another random parking lot? But a white dually with a trailer and two sets of blue tarps is a thing easily remembered. Even by this oblivious asshole of the road. Nessy's Barbecue Barn offered several places to pull a rig like his out of immediate sight and the man was glad about that. But he needed fuel even worse than the black SUV did and so he had to execute multiple errands during this stop and see to them in careful stages.

The man elected to drive his rig past the establishment in order to appear casual while formulating a plan. From the road he could see the gold New Orleans helmet sticker occupying Pump 1 on the south fuel island in front of the main entrance. Of course he was there. He had to back into the lane against the intended traffic flow so that the gas cap on the black SUV could face the pump. The hoses were clearly long enough to stretch across to the opposite side but that would require effort and also courtesy. Oh, how he hated this man.

Every time the man in the white dually felt his resolve beginning to slip, the black SUV asshole would provide him with enough fresh offenses to keep the thing going. He was making it too easy, in fact.

The man in the white dually spotted another island of pumps on the east side of the building. The property was bordered on the north by an unmanned carwash and this was his point of entry. He pulled into the carwash lot and circled behind the empty spray stalls and then drove south to the east fuel pump island at Nessy's Barbecue Barn. Perfectly aligned to the traffic arrows and even his extended trailer offered no obstacle to other potential customers. But since he carried no plastic anymore, the man had to go inside to prepay for his gasoline with cash. Another risk of discovery, but not much of one.

No doubt Mr. Black SUV paid with his debit card and then pressed the button offering a receipt and then pitched the receipt into the little trash receptacle with the squeegee-well filled with bluish fluid and then pulled into the closest parking space available and then headed straight for the men's room to relieve himself perhaps in multiple ways and then failed to wash his hands afterward and then immediately seated himself in the dining hall and then began scouring the menu for the most obnoxious dinner entree available during lunch hours. Thus he'd be too preoccupied to stack any random and unlikely familiarities together. Besides. Neither man had made any direct eye contact up to this point. He was probably safe enough.

The owner of the white dually went inside the restaurant and found an impressive convenience store tucked away to the right side. Bit of Christmas decoration thrown up here and there. All new and all disposable. Santa chalked onto the inside plate glass with a Nessy's logo on his sled. Two clerks worked cash registers and this was clearly the place to prepay for gas if a person were still antiquated enough to exchange foldable currency for services rendered. This he did. He also bought a pack of gum and a red sports drink. Behind the clerks the man could see his rig through the plate glass still at the pumps and he felt some satisfaction at its skillful positioning. This world would be so different if people only thought of others more than they do. Such an easy thing too.

He left four twenties on the counter and told the shorter clerk he would be back for his change after he fueled up and parked. The clerk nodded his springy ginger hair.

"Sure thing, boss. And Happy Holidays." He did not look up. Couldn't be bothered to do so. This world. This damn world.

The man went out to the east pumps and filled his gas tank. The cost was above seventy-two dollars and this was also a symptom of something. He thought about the owner of the black SUV. He wondered how that man would exit Nessy's Barbecue Barn after defiling himself with an embarrassing excess of food. He would be smugly satisfied and just a bit uncomfortable. Both conditions played to the advantage of the man owning the white dually. There was no reason to expect his target to be preoccupied with his surroundings. But that only reduced the risk of discovery without eliminating it entirely. Random things that should never happen happen all the time.

From the east pumps he could not see the main entrance at all and this was another advantage. The same had to be true in reverse. Totally hidden right where he was. This was a good side to leave his conspicuous rig. In fact this was the only safe side, the more he considered it. The other man would stumble out to his clichéd vehicle and pull around to the left and then onto the street and the closest opportunity for a U-turn was a traffic light some two blocks to the north. By the time the black SUV could aim itself towards the I-55 onramp its driver would have long forgotten all about Nessy's Barbecue Barn other than being the likely source of his oncoming indigestion. He would probably blame them for his gastrointestinal discomfort and then give them a bad review in retaliation.

The man parked his white dually along the east wall and went inside the building and found his change waiting on him and his opinion of the ginger clerk improved slightly before the encounter disappeared from his memory forever.

He went to the hostess station and surveyed the room for the man he saw at the Eat Good All Day diner in Jackson Mississippi. It took a minute. The hostess came over and the man held up his hand asking for just a little more time. Then he spotted him. The man owning the black SUV was seated at a table with four chairs and against the showcase window. Immediate disgust.

"Ma'am. See that table over yonder by the widows?" She did. "I'd like to sit two tables on this side of that one if I can." She assured him that he could sit there or anywhere else that suited him. She led him to the table and handed him a large menu in a vinyl maroon trifold encasement. He sat down and asked for water.

The other man was further along in the lunching process. He was buttering a roll and he appeared to be drinking iced tea. Had he ordered any sort of alcoholic beverage his pursuer likely would have snapped right there inside Nessy's Barbecue Barn and beaten him to death with whatever happened to be handy and thus our story would end in Memphis. But the other man did not order so much as one beer. Points for that.

No, said the noise. No points for that. Failing to the break the law is hardly a cause for handing out awards. That's what's wrong with everything. People waiting on parades for barely doing what should be expected of everyone. The bar is so low now. Remember what he really is. You know what he really is.

A waitress came to his table and the noise again ebbed itself away from the shores of his weather-beaten mind.

"Know what you want, sir?"

He was hungry now and the fact annoyed him.

"Um. Yes. The uh... brisket sandwich. No sides. Glass of sweet tea. Please."

"No mac n cheese? No beans? Comes with and you pay for it either way." She laughed and rolled her eyes at the injustice of combination pricing.

"No sides. Thanks."

"Lemon with the tea?"

"No lemon. Just tea. Sweet."

She scratched some in-house code on her notepad and then stepped outside the boundaries of his peripheral vision.

During his own lunch-ordering process the lunch for the man two tables ahead had arrived. Ribs. Big slathery ribs and what looked to be a full rack of them. And two sets of sloppy side items spilling over the plate and onto the table. A full slab of ribs. For lunch. While driving the first leg of an extended road trip. And after having eaten T-bone steak and eggs some three hours before.

This boundless gluttony surprised even the man who hated the eater already. Such waste. So unnecessary. Had we dedicated an entire lifetime to giving ourselves everything we want and as much as we want and exactly at the moment we want it? The disgusted man almost pitied the other man. To be so enslaved by the basest impulses. How horrible it must be to need everything and yet experience fulfillment in nothing.

He looked at the man's obesity showcased beyond both sides of his overmatched wicker chair and the owner of the white dually shook his head. Little wonder, he thought. Eat like that at every meal and you're just begging your body to give up on you. Maybe what he thought to be a vendetta and a reckoning was in fact euthanasia. Maybe the mission bouncing around inside his head and fueled by relentless noise was an act of kindness in disguise. This other man was clearly suffering whether he was cognizant of it or not. Even that man did not deserve this level of endless torment. He owed a debt certainly but just look at him. He didn't owe this much. What an awful life.

The waitress returned to the table with his brisket sandwich and sides of mac n cheese and baked beans. Since they were included in the price either way. He looked up at her.

"I just couldn't let you waste them, honey. You're paying for them anyway."

"But now you've made sure I'll waste them. I am not going to eat them and now you can't serve them to anyone else. So now they will be thrown away untouched. How is that not wasteful?"

"Well, when you put it that way. You should try them. Both of em. They're real good."

He looked up at her. Again a noise buzzed around inside his skull but this noise was not as loud as other similar noises. He pursed his lips.

"Thank you, ma'am. I'm good. I'll take the check whenever you have it handy."

She tore off his ticket and laid it on the table. Since payment was accepted at the register he hoped never to see this woman again. And he never did. He took one bite of his brisket sandwich and it was good. But the man did not want to eat anymore. Lost his appetite altogether. He laid the sandwich back down in the green plastic basket with the checkered napkin. He gave the basket a flick with his right hand and his meal moved several inches further away. A heavy sigh. He looked at the man who had ordered the ribs and he was surprised by what he saw.

The man who owned the new black SUV was not eating his slathery ribs. Instead he was sobbing and trying not to sob but he was powerless to help himself. Why was he sobbing? How does a guy like him screw up enough emotion to cry over anything? Unless you punch him in the mouth, of course. Then he'd sit down and bawl like a baby, no doubt. The owner of the white dually scanned the room. It was unlikely that anyone else had punched him. Maybe he just needed a good punch. Maybe that was what was wrong with him, big picture. But that was not what was wrong with him at the moment. Something else was bothering him. He was trying to stifle himself and he was wiping his face with checkered napkins. No one else at Nessy's seemed to notice how upset this man was nor how hard he was trying to regain composure. The man sitting behind the rejected brisket sandwich was baffled completely.

Then he remembered. In Jackson this man had told complete strangers that his mom was dying and this was the reason for his road trip to Chicago. Could this be the reason for his emotional breakdown? Was his mom really in the dying process? Did he actually love her to the point of weeping? The man assumed the other man was exaggerating at best just to momentarily impress people he would never care about. But was it true? Could an inconsiderate gluttonous pig also love his momma and tend to her during her final hours? Was this a good son or a bad son?

Or maybe none of that had anything to do with the crying. Maybe that guy had just found out he lost a bet and owed his bookie more than he could pay and now he expected a leg breaking. Maybe his stocks took a nosedive. Who knows? Who cares? Still an asshole only now he's a blubbering asshole. More disgust. What would his daddy think seeing him bawl like this?

The owner of the white dually took his ticket to the register and paid for his sandwich and also the sides because they were included in the price either way. Unlike the breakfast encounter in Jackson he did not pay for the other man's lunch. Witnessing the stifled sobbing was satisfaction enough whether he could identify the reason or not.

He left Nessy's Barbecue Barn and climbed into his truck and started the engine and he began waiting but he did not have to wait for very long. Soon he saw the black SUV exit the lot and head up the street towards the light where a U-turn could be negotiated. No reason to hurry now. Both men knew where that black SUV was headed. After allowing for what seemed to be a sensible cushion, the man in the while dually pulled his rig forward. They continued heading north on I-55.

When Caring Crosses Over into Meddling

His phone kept ringing. He put it on vibrate and then it ran itself around in little circles atop the cushion of the passenger seat inside the white dually. He knew who was calling. There weren't many options left these days.

Collection agencies were a part of everyday life and he almost considered their detailed threats a form of company. He had nothing left to repo so let them say whatever they wanted. Want my truck and my trailer? Come take em. Why not? I can't stand the sight of them anyway. Sometimes he insisted on engaging in meaningless chitchat with the representatives and they had no idea what to do with him.

"Sir, we called you last week and advised you that this was your last opportunity to make arrangements for settling your account. I'm afraid that deadline has passed and you are still delinquent."

"John, is it? What's for dinner tonight, John?"

"I don't think you quite grasp the situation, sir. This is quite serious."

"It's Tuesday, I think. There's a great Taco Tuesday special here in my town. Mom and pop place. Buy three and get two for free. How you like that? Do you have anything like that up your way? Wherever you are, I mean."

"Sir, we do have the power to garnishee your wages. Brite Star Staffing Service where you are currently employed is aware of your obligations and they have assured us they will cooperate."

"Are you a crispy taco man, John? I know I am. Never understood the fascination with soft tacos. Want a burrito just order a burrito. Right? What's the point?"

"Good evening, sir. I'm sorry we could not reach an understanding. We'll be in touch."

"Please do! Same time tomorrow night? Wednesdays are good nights for fried chicken. Do you like fried chicken, John?"

[Click]

He looked forward to such calls. His buddy Spam Risk had been calling with increased regularity but he or she were never much fun. Spammy never seemed to know who he or she was talking to and the man in the white dually much preferred adversaries who did their homework. But neither of these camps were calling him just now.

There was one person left who knew all his pain and had walked through life with him and therefore could see through his bullshit no matter how much glitter he tried to sprinkle over the top of it. It was her alright. He knew this because he had assigned that specific ringtone to her alone and she was the last person he wanted to talk to at present and so he silenced his cellphone altogether. But now it buzzed and danced and buzzed and damn she was stubborn though. Why was she calling today? How did she know? Somehow she always knows. Just like Santa.

She didn't live nearby. New Mexico and up in the mountains. She didn't know about his eviction or his modest pile of cash or his liquidated life scattered over two vehicles covered with blue tarps and she certainly had no idea what he was up to right now. What was he up to right now? It buzzed again. She did know everything else. All the rest of it and in great detail. That made her far more intimidating than any collection agent or any outsourced scam artist seeking access to his empty bank accounts. And she was far more persistent.

Fine, he said. He concentrated on trying to sound normal, whatever that was. Practiced out loud twice. He picked up his phone and took a deep breath and he answered the call.

"Sis! How's it going? How's George?"

"How's George? What's going on?"

Damnit. Overplayed.

"What do you mean? Can't a guy ask about his brother-in-law?"

"Not this guy and not that brother-in-law. Never mind. Listen. I've been thinking about you a lot today. I know the anniversary is getting close and I don't want you to be alone for it. Speaking of George, I told him I wanted to be with you in Louisiana for a few days. He said he'd watch the kids while I was gone."

"He what?"

"Don't be an ass. He understands. Give him that much credit at least. So anyway. I should be there day after tomorrow. Are you working?"

"Oh. Yeah. About that. Um. Listen Betty. Coming to visit isn't really gonna work for me right now."

"I wasn't asking."

"You never do. And you also never listen. But right now would be a great time to do both. I'm not even in Louisiana right now."

"What? Well where the hell are you then? It sounds like you're driving. Are you driving? Did you find a big job?"

"Yeah you could say that. The biggest job I've had in years basically fell right into my lap as a matter of fact. I'm actually on my way there now. Needed my trailer and everything. Chicago, if you can believe that."

"Um. I really can't believe that. Chicago? And during the holidays? What? Why you? No offense but don't they have plenty of drywallers in Illinois? Why you and why all the way up there?"

"Rude! Thanks for the support, sis."

"Sorry! I just mean..."

"I know. Fair question. Brite Star put me onto it if you must know. They have branches all over the central U.S. including Illinois, thank you very much. Anyway they posted this job on the website. Finishing out some big office building and they're subbing out everything. I really don't know anything more about it than the square footage. But you know I'm kinda ready to see some new things. You can appreciate that probably. Anyway I fired off a bid and even with my travel expenses and having to hire a couple a locals to help me lift and mud and tape, I still got the job."

"What does that tell you?"

"Well, two things: those Chicago drywallers must really overbid their jobs and also my sister in Taos is a smart ass."

"Ha ha. Funny. You're really just randomly driving to Chicago to work some drywall job in some office building? Right before Christmas? Wild. How long will you be gone?"

"Nothing random about it. Christmas in Corsequette is not my idea of a great time these days. Maybe you can appreciate that if you stop long enough to give it a think. Besides. Make hay while the sun shines and right now it shines way up and to the north. How long, I can't say. Who knows? If I like it I just might stay."

"Oh, the hell you will. Well. I guess I'm glad you're keeping yourself busy and I'm glad you've found some work. You can always ask if you need a little help, you know. Or you could come and stay with us for a while if you want. At least through the new year. Maybe into the spring even. Fishing is great up here! I know, I know. We've been over this a million times. I'll be thinking about you next week. Please call me if you think of it. Okay? I'm worried about you."

"I know. And thanks. I'll be okay. Tell Fartbreath I said to have a holly jolly Christmas."

"He loves you too. Bye."

There was zero chance any of that story would hold together for very long. Not with Betty. He knew he never should have answered that call. Where was good ol' Spam Risk when you needed him or her.

No Disposable Moments (Part I)

On this morning breakfast was not altogether different than it had been on countless mornings before it. But there was never another one like it during the days and weeks and months and years that followed after. Christmas three days away. Life was steady then by comparison. Happy and dull and taken for granted and collectively a Petri dish for culturing the sort of grouchy and pissy attitude only permissible within the confines of absolute love and absolute safety. In the absence of substantive conflict nearly any basic annoyance will attempt to fill the vacuum. Today it was eggs and their preparation. And long-established cooking preferences that should have been absorbed and assimilated into rote routine by now. We were way past the point of requiring instructions. And yet we weren't. It was a problem.

"Damnit Rhonda!" he said. "You broke the yokes. Really?"

"I did? Sorry babe." She wasn't sorry enough.

"Are you? I kinda doubt it. Do you know what it's like slinging those wallboards every day? With my back? Who's gonna help me? Joey? Marco? They can't hardly lift a drill or even the screws. I can't do this forever but I'll keep going till I keel over one day, I guess. Count on that. Why I got into this dead-end business I'll never know but here I am. Fine. All I need to make it through another day is a little protein. Bacon and eggs and maybe a bit of cheese. That's all I ask. And after all these years you still don't seem to know I like them sunny side up. How? Such a small thing to ask. Those little suns are about all I look forward to each morning. I don't know why they lift me up but they do. Is that so hard? I've told you this."

"Got it. You want suns. Easy, Icarus," she said. He couldn't remember who Icarus was and so now she was flaunting her education in his face. Calling him stupid. How much of this shit was he supposed to take? "I tried to cook them like you like them but I guess I screwed up. Again. Sue me. Cook your own damn eggs next time."

"Why do you have to be so dramatic? All I said was I like sunny side up eggs and you already know that."

"You're right. Totally my fault. What's really on your mind?"

"What are you saying? Being denied a decent breakfast no matter how hard I work isn't enough to get me frustrated right now?"

"That is exactly what I am saying. Yes. What's bothering you?"

He wanted to be angry but he wasn't angry. She was right and he knew it and he loved her and all of it together really pissed him off in an utterly childish and useless way and now he wanted somehow to save face but saw no pathway to do so. It was time to stop and he knew it and he also knew he needed to apologize even if experiencing actual remorse was still several minutes into the future.

"You're right. Sorry. It's the bill collectors. On and on and on and on with these assholes. The best of them maybe gives two shits. When we lost the skating rink we lost the big job I needed to finally catch us up for good. Every time it's right in my grasp it slips away again. I don't know how to fix it or get ahead of it. You know? There's always some other bill or some other permit or some extra expense or something breaks down and damnit. It wasn't supposed be like this, Rhonda. This was supposed to be our big chance. We were supposed to be free and clear by now and we're still at least six months away from seeing any relief at all. Six months! At best, I mean."

"So what's six months? What were we doing six months ago?" She counted on her fingers. "June, right? Might as well have been a minute ago. Last Christmas seems like yesterday. Remember last Christmas? Betty was here trying to run things like she does. You know. Remember how she had to be Santa? Gifts had to go out from under the tree in a certain order? You know how much order always means to her. Ha! Anyway that was not so long ago really. And June was half that, baby. So what are we talking about now?" She counted on her fingertips again but forward this time. "Lookee there. June is six months ahead just the same as it is six months behind. Be here before you know it. Summer always gets here sooner rather than later. You know that. If that's all the time we need to finally break even then that's good news. Actually start getting ahead by fall? Shit. After all we've been through? What's another six months? I'm good with it! Why aren't you?"

She picked up the spent dishes and the irrelevant unused dishes from the table and took them to the sink. He looked down at his coffee. It was still swirling from his incessant stirring even though the sugar had long since dissolved. A nervous tick of sorts. If he could have dug down into the earth's core by scraping through that earthen, blueish-glazed cup he'd have gladly done so. Why not? What's another seismic eruption? Instead all he could do was clink away aimlessly and stare into the swirling and overly sweet blackness searching for answers that even the richest coffee beans could never supply. He looked up at Melissa in her highchair. Two years old already. How?

"What do you say, Melissa? Are we gonna make it after all? I mean, when summer gets here?"

Melissa offered no advice. She instead played with her banana-based breakfast mush using a ducky spoon as a backhoe bucket and guided a bit of the lumpy paste towards the general vicinity of her unsuspecting mouth. Some of its nutrients likely made their way into her stomach by happenstance and this was considered a resounding victory. She smiled and giggled and it appeared to all in attendance that she was somehow enjoying her accidental breakfast. The giggles. He loved being her daddy. He loved the giggles. Be like this forever, he thought. Be exactly like this and never change.

"Okay. Sorry I was pissy, honey. I'm gone. Finishing out Gumtree Estates this week. What's your day look like?" He slurped downed the dregs of his cooling sweet black coffee.

"Not much. I have to go to the market today. Melissa and me. She's a great shopper. Very shrewd with coupons."

He looked at her. Her finger was in her nose.

"I bet she is. You girls have fun."

Out the door he went.

The memory ended right there. All memories ended right there. The needle lifted from the groove in the vinyl and though the record beneath spun on, no sound escaped the speakers except a faint electronic hum mixing with the vast and endless apathetic silence of life afterward. If only he could have stopped all of spacetime in that moment. Why not? Nothing in the expanding universe could ever eclipse that singularity. Surely whatever inhabited worlds there might be scrolled across the far-flung galaxies would agree. Maybe the Big Bang functioned only to give rise to this improbable bit of perfection. Stop everything and right here and right now and congratulations all around. This was it. Well done.

But time did not stop and this moment was gone and it was exactly as fleeting as all other moments. And then he was back inside his white dually pulling his former drywaller's trailer. Blue tarps stretched across both and secured with failing bungee cables.

"He is exactly like him," he said. "Whether he knows it or not."

Up ahead some 200 yards a black SUV with a gold helmet decal on the rear windshield bobbed in and out of traffic as if the rest of the motorists on I-55 were lesser beings driven on by lesser impulses. The man in the white dually narrowed his gaze. He hated that man so much. More with each passing mile marker.

The Second of Three Unpleasant Phone Calls

It was time for an update on his mom's condition. The man had spoken to the on-call nurse the night before and her vital signs were not improving. He had no reason to believe today would be any different but there were now practical matters in play. Mortality has its own timeline and it seldom appreciates the logistical needs of the living. He was starting to get the hang of his bluetooth dashboard controls nearly to the point of appreciating their value. He scrolled through his contacts until reaching Pleasant Latter Days Skilled Nursing and he placed the call. He reached the front desk and they knew his voice by now.

"Pleasant Latter Days, can you hold?"

This is never truly a question.

"Yes." On came the hold music. Eventually Barbara picked up the line.

"Sorry for your wait. Can I help you?"

"Barbara? This is Violet's son. Violet in room 116. Remember me?"

"Oh sure, honey. How can I help you?"

"Hi. Can you patch me through to the on-call nurse for today? It's the weekend so I'm guessing Rebecca is here today. Is that right?"

"No, dear. She is out with a bug. Gloria is on today. Do you know Gloria?"

"Gloria. Sure I know her. Can I speak to her?"

"We're really slammed today. But if you don't mind waiting I'll page her."

He did not mind. What else did he have to do? He passed three mile markers before Gloria reengaged the call holding on Line Two. In the interim a lovely clarinet interpretation of a familiar jazz song the title of which he could not quite place played over his new car stereo, patronizing him for an extra measure of patience. The tune was instantly recognizable and yet he did not know a single lyric or even the title. How was this possible? Was it something about a woman and a town? Montevideo was it? He assumed that once a skilled wordsmith had carefully crafted all of the accompanying lyrics with painstaking attention to precision and clarity and now none of that craftsmanship mattered at all. The words and their collective meaning might as well have never existed in any practical sense. Gone forever into the unforgiving ether of indifference and relentless hurry. And yet the melodic bedding stripped of any contextual significance was nonetheless piping away into his factory surround speakers as he traveled north on I-55 at least fifty years after the song's publication. Everyone involved in its creation was likely long deceased and apparently it had all been for this.

Here he was barely listening to their climatic achievement while awaiting a grim update on his mom's own journey along the dying process. There was zero chance that any of the song's composers, whomever they might have been, had this in mind while they were banging away at an upright piano in some rehearsal hall and drafting forgotten stanzas onto a notepad. He thought about all of this while he waited for Gloria to make her way to the nurses' station and the whole of it was somewhat unsettling and very depressing in a way that it should not have been. He remembered it is only a song after all. A buttress against absolute silence. Maybe they wrote the song for this moment. Who can say why anything ever happens? Most art never serves any tangible purpose and by definition. He was thankful for their gift whether they intended to give it to him specifically or not. And it did extend his patience somehow. Where the hell is Montevideo anyway?

"This is Gloria."

"Gloria? Hi! This is Violet's son. From Baton Rouge? Do you remember me?"

"Of course. How are you?'

"I'm fine. Fine. How is Mom today?"

"No positive changes, I'm afraid. In fact things are looking worse. Your mom is never awake unless we wake her and then she goes right back to sleep as soon as we leave. She is refusing to eat or drink. We come to her bedside twice a day and try to coax her into some simple physical therapy but she just turns her head to the opposite side and waits for us to leave. When we tell her she has to eat she just nods her head and says she understands. Then she refuses even her applesauce. She's starting to take on fluid in her legs too. I hate to be the one to tell you this but I think we're down to days, if not hours. I don't think she wants to be here anymore, sweetie. Can you come see her?"

"I'm on my way. Please tell her that for me?"

"Sure I will. I'll tell her. That will help. I think she's holding on for you. If you want to know the truth."

Silent and slow tears.

"I'm coming as fast as I can get there. I'll be at Latter Days by noon tomorrow."

"Very good. Listen. We were going to call you anyway. Her BP is starting to slip and we don't like some of the signs we're seeing today. If she gets worse it will all happen very fast. Tell me your wishes. Would you like us to get her to a hospital or would you like us to let her slip away here in her room? Damn. I hate putting it like that. Anyway..."

"Try to save her as long as you can! I know we have a DNR but other than that if a hospital has a chance you need to let them try. Send her if it comes to that, Gloria. Please!"

"Okay. Okay. We will. Promise. Please get here as fast as you can though. This is not an exact science and we are talking about end of life now. Weeks. Days. Hours. Only God knows. But it will be soon. She is so tired."

"Thank you, Gloria. I'm coming and I'll be there tomorrow. Bless you and bless all of you who care for her." He was fully choked up and the words fought to form themselves against his trembling throat. "I love her so much and I have tried my best. You know?"

"I do know. We all know. She knows. Even if she will not say it I know she loves you very much. That's a tough lady in that bed and Death has his hands full. But do hurry. She's holding on but she cannot fight it much longer. We're all very proud of your mother."

"I'm proud of Mom too. Thank you, Gloria. I'll see you by lunchtime tomorrow. Goodbye."

He ended the call by touching the red tab on his dashboard interface. Then he began sobbing for a variety of reasons. The woman Gloria was describing did not match the mom he had ever known. But knowing his father like he did it did not surprise him that if love were ever to be expressed it could only happen from a distance and likely through indirect mediums.

The point was she loved him. Had he ever heard her say as much? Hard to remember specifically. While he never doubted it on an implicit level he was somehow surprised to now have even inferential evidence confirming the fact. Maybe Gloria was merely saying the things people in her position are supposed to say in such times, but he made a choice to accept her testimony as delivered.

His mom loved him. She had always loved him. Even her biting sarcasm made sense now. And he would repay her love by being by her side during her final hours and during her ultimate transition. He would get there for her. Nothing else mattered. He would hold her hand and let her know that her only child loved her to the very end and she could pass on knowing that she was loved and would be missed and would always be remembered and he understood her at last. It. All of it. Was okay now. Who could want more from this life than to know everything was finally okay just before whatever happens after finally happens? When no time is left to screw everything up all over again. Such peace would be gold rendering the wealth of Solomon roughly on par with spent tin cans and sundry jagged scrap.

He clicked off his cruise control and reengaged the application at six miles above the posted speed limit. Let them come at him with their radar guns and their ticket books. If the offended officer ever loved his or her momma he or she would quickly understand his urgency. He had to get his ass to Chicago before lunchtime tomorrow. Maybe he could feed her pudding or help her drink some protein and maybe just being there would help. Maybe it would indeed.

The Last of Three Unpleasant Phone Calls

This call wasn't likely to be unpleasant so much as it had the potential to become tiresome and even testy if the man driving the black SUV had run out of patience for the day. But he took his own mental temperature and reckoned he probably had enough patience left in reserve to navigate one more. He took a deep breath and he placed the call.

His mom had a cousin in Aurora Illinois. The two women had not been exactly close for some time and they were even less so these days. Different lives forever spinning farther away along different arcs. But they had grown up together and had maintained somewhat regular contact over the years. They certainly loved each other after a peculiar and nostalgic fashion. That was the upside to calling Judith. There was also a downside.

The man driving the black SUV understood his second cousin placed enormous value on his mom's assorted piles of useless and overly sentimental crap. The same junk that made his skin crawl was somehow extremely important to Judith. Why, he could not imagine. This priority disappointed him and exhausted him, but he was not exactly sure why it bothered him to the extent that it did. Taken the whole way round, piles of useless clutter under one roof or under another roof instead really should not move the needle all that much. So why did he care? Maybe it came down to timing.

Personally, the man driving the black SUV found the practice of scavenging over the artifacts of the dead or of the not quite dead utterly tasteless. It bothered him immensely whenever any discussion veered off in that direction and this made calling Cousin Judith a dicey situation. None of this bothered her one bit. He knew when he called Judith she would not be able to help herself. Yet for all her tacky list-making the driver of the black SUV knew she loved his mom and he knew her heart was in the right place. So he also knew Judith was owed a phone call to inform her that his mom's time was drawing near. He loved Judith too and very much. They talked often. If only he could keep her out of that corner. Sigh. Unlikely.

"Hey you."

"Hey. How are you? I wish I had good news."

"Oh no. Your mom? How is she, sweetheart?"

"Not good. I'm trying to get there as fast as I can. But they haven't moved Baton Rouge any closer to Chicago so I won't get up there until lunchtime tomorrow. And only then if I push it. Which I am. Have you talked to her?"

"Not for a month or so. She didn't sound all that great then but I didn't see this coming. Not this soon at least. Where are you now?"

"About 125 miles north of Memphis. Stopping in St. Louis tonight and then I'll be up and out before dawn. Do you think you can call them and give them your number? Just in case she gets worse. In a pinch you can get to her a lot quicker than I can. I hate to put this on you. But..."

"Never mind. I love your mom. You know that. I'll call right away. And I'll meet you over there tomorrow if you'd like."

"Thanks, Judith."

"Has she mentioned what she wants to do with her walnut cabinet for knickknacks? She doesn't have anything in it right now except pictures in frames and such."

Here we go.

"No. We haven't talked about any of that."

"I'm sure. There are so many more important things to sort out! I know that. It's just that I have my collection of bisque and ceramic robin figurines. Remember? And they would look great in that cabinet. Every time I look at them I will think of your mother. What

79

a great memorial to her memory. My robins on display in her honor. Don't you think?"

"I don't know. I guess. I haven't thought about her furniture yet. She's still alive and all."

"Of course you haven't! Neither have I. But the dying often take comfort in knowing that their belongings are going places where they will be loved and cherished forever. You know?"

"That's interesting. If I were dying I doubt I'd care where my mahogany knickknack cabinet was headed next."

"I think it's walnut. But, good. At least I can take this much off your plate. Can I help you with anything else? Her home is full of so many wonderful memories and it will be a burden to sort through them all. You know what they mean to her. Would you like my help?"

"Maybe. I don't know. Not today. But would you mind calling Pleasant Latter Days just in case something happens? I'll get there as quickly as I can but I can't get there before the morning. And if I did I'd be no good to anyone anyway. I'm gonna need a bit of sleep at least. I love you, Judith. Thanks for loving my mom too."

"Of course! Loved her longer than you have, you know. And I love you too. You drive safe, okay? I'll see you tomorrow."

"Okay. I'll see you tomorrow."

"Bye, hon."

The phone went dead and his current playlist resumed annexation of his factory surround sound. He was worn out now, utterly and completely. Walnut cabinet. Two hundred miles yet to St. Louis. His unpleasant calls were thus ended and he was now free to stare blankly ahead and let the numbing miles and the broken white line on the pavement pull him northward towards a few hours of broken rest.

Of Course She Couldn't Let It Go

Betty called him back. Of course she did. Big sisters who loved unconditionally were always this way. At least his sister had always been this way. She never knew when she was crossing any sort of line and she crossed them all the time.

Betty had a gift for making shit worse than it already was and always fueled by best intentions. Example: you don't really escape bullies by having your big sister throw them a beatdown on their way home from school. Bullies tend to remember encounters like that and in unflattering context. You don't get to be a bully by being a weakling in disguise or by picking on victims who could actually kick your ass if properly motivated. Stand up for yourself and vengeance is coming even if it is delayed. This is even more true if any spasmodic fit of insurrection is championed by your obnoxious and boisterous older sister. There are rules where girls are concerned but these rules won't save you. The driver of the white dually had a scar on his head where no hair would grow. Four staples. But he was not being bullied today and he wasn't the one in need of saving.

Something very different was happening. If she knew what was really going on, would she still interfere? More than ever. Certainly. Go away, Betty. Stop calling me, Betty. Butt out for once in your damn life, Betty. I got this, Betty. He put the phone to his ear.

"Hey, Betty!"

"Um hum. I've been looking into Brite Star and don't be mad at me! But I don't see any jobs board that lets you bid on jobs, even locally. Much less in faraway places like Chicago. What is really going on, brother?"

"Oh!" he said. "Are you now a member of the Brite Star Staffing team? I had no idea! Welcome, Big Sister!"

"Don't be an ass. You've always been an ass as a matter of fact. No. I don't work for Brite Star. So what? I'm not talking about that and you damn well know it. Whatever you're doing doesn't make any sense and I can smell it all the way from here. What are you really up to?"

"Explain, sister."

"Eat a turd, brother. You know what I'm talking about so don't play coy with me. You have never left Corsequette Louisiana even before the accident and now suddenly you're driving all the way up to Chicago during the holidays to stay for God knows how long to do a job that five hundred other locals could do without your travel expenses and duh. I just don't buy it!"

"Damn, Betty. So glad I have you to fact check all my stories for me. Okay. If I'm not headed to Chicago to drywall an office complex then do tell me: what am I really doing? Wait! I'll pull over onto the shoulder so I can get on the edge of my seat." He kept driving and she knew he was mocking her. "Just a minute! Hold on. There! Okay. Now I'm in park on the shoulder of the interstate. I can't wait! Why. Exactly. Am I headed up to Chicago if not for a drywall job? I'll wait because this theory of yours has to be good."

"And. Kiss my ass."

"No. Go on."

"I don't know what you're up to. Okay? That's exactly the problem. I know you have never left Corsequette Louisiana to take a drywall job. Not even for other cities still within Kissisaw Parish. Now you're suddenly headed up to Chicago Illinois of all places and none of this makes any sense at all. I don't believe you could bid a job so low that the locals couldn't beat your price plus travel. I have run the numbers and there is no way. I've even called a couple of drywallers in Chicago and taken bids on fictitious jobs and they come in at more or less with the same estimates you charge. And this is without allowing for travel."

"You're getting real-time bids over the phone for jobs in Chicago and on a Saturday no less? Impressive! Need a job, sis?"

"Just tell me you're meeting an escort up in Chicago and I'll forget all about it on purpose. You could use some friendly company and I wouldn't blame you. But I need to know something besides what you're telling me or I can't let it go. I'm about to fly out to Chicago myself and see to my little brother like I always have. So make this easier on both of us and spill it. Right now! Use your words."

"What? No!"

"No what? No you aren't spending your money on an escort or no you won't spill whatever it is you're up to or no you don't want me coming up to Chicago and learning everything you won't tell me?"

"Um. Gross! A prostitute! You know I would never!"

"We're both adults. Life has played you the shittiest of hands. I'm sorry for that. I know you have to be lonely and I would never judge you."

"Oh my God, sis. I'm not going to Chicago to meet up with an escort. Okay? Just... Ew! How could you? I told you I have a job to do and I intend to do it. If you want to fly to O'Hare and then rent a car only to watch me slather mud onto wallboard in downtown Chicago that's your business. But I feel like you'll regret wasting the money. Stay in Taos with Georgie and my nieces and have a Merry Christmas and I'll call you whenever I get back to Corsequette. Damn, sis. An escort? Driving up to Chicago to meet up with an escort. Is that me? Really? Would I ever do that to Rhonda? Think about what you're saying."

"Well, no. I know better. But I can't make sense of this so I'm grasping at straws. Okay? What do you expect? I mean, I wouldn't blame you if you needed some friendly company."

"Is this about me or about you, Betty?"

"Yep, I knew it. You're an asshole. I love you and goodbye. Prick."

The phone went dead.

But her brother was not the asshole. The asshole was driving the black SUV up ahead of him some 350 yards or so. Betty had sounded her retreat but not an unconditional surrender. She'd rally eventually like all his previous bullies had always done before her.

What did she know about anything anyway? George was still by her side and so were his nieces Sara and Emily. How bad could life really be for any of them? People who have never lost anything worth losing always seem to know how utterly defeated people should respond to Ground Zero. His Ground Zero arrived six months ago in the form of his lowest pit of depression, some eighteen months after his life collapsed forever. Meanwhile she was enjoying life with George and Sara and Emily in Taos New Mexico with world-class fly-fishing excursions and excellent local food. And that was perfect. But since then things had gotten much worse. Her little brother had stepped several existential flights further downward, past depression and grief and towards a vengeful and howling abyss, and now he was looking back up at Ground Zero with equal parts envy and despair.

Betty loved him but Betty could never understand him. And he did not want Betty to understand him because he loved Betty also. She needed to remember who he used to be and remain a spectator cheering for him on the sidelines and never hear the noise ricocheting around inside his skull. He was far away now. Dark days across a failing bridge and with barely a lantern flickering off in the distance to guide him back home. The good news was at least that feeble light yet burned on in spite of the howling winds. A single flame inside his chest remained, a flame every bit as stubborn as Betty herself.

Pleasant Last Day

The man in the black SUV was now driving towards the southern outskirts of St. Louis. It had been dark for a long time already. Too many stops along the way and too much time spent at each stop. He should have made better time driving on a Saturday even during the holidays. Driving all the way from Baton Rouge to Chicago in one day is not practical and even if he made himself do that he would not have made it to Pleasant Latter Days Skilled Nursing in time for a visit until the next morning. Every plan he could think of still required two days of travel.

He could have flown but then he would not have had his own vehicle. The days ahead would require a lot of moving and shuttling of clutter and heaps of antiquated paperwork and supposed keepsakes and other such debris. Donation hubs and landfills and maybe even a small storage unit but he hoped not. His new black SUV would be much handier for these deliveries than whatever rental he might have found available during the holidays in Chicago. Flying was out. Only driving made sense and thus he was effectively right on time, so the plan was proving to be a solid one. But it still bothered him to be no further along than he was at present.

Maybe it was the memory of his granddad on road trips. He would sooner hand you a coffee can than pull into a rest area. Making good time was everything in those days regardless of other factors. Maybe it was the miles he had put in by this time. Hard driving even with extended stops. He was spent and he wanted out of that damn black SUV and away from that damn GPS second guessing every lane change. So tired and so cranky now. A notification on his dashboard suggested he stop for a coffee break.

He was glad to know his Tremendous 10 was roughly forty-five minutes away although that still sounded like thirty minutes too many. He had made sure to reserve a room at the northern-most location in St. Louis along I-55. Bit of a built-in head start towards Chicago for whenever morning came, but morning was still hours away.

A call came in on his dashboard interface. His contacts recognized the number. Pleasant Latter Days Skilled Nursing. He knew what they were going to tell him before he answered. They knew he would be there by lunchtime tomorrow so apparently this news could not wait. Judith had undoubtedly called them by now. Days or hours, Gloria had said. Days or hours. A good son a bad son.

"Yes. This is Violet Reynolds' son. Go ahead."

"Mr. Reynolds. It's Gloria again. Sir. Your mom is sleeping but we can't rouse her anymore. We are noticing some changes in your mom's breathing too. It has become very rapid and shallow. At times she'll pause and then a big gasp. Sir, I cannot predict the future, of course. However I have guided residents through this process many times and I think we are very close now. I would be very surprised if she is still with us by tomorrow. Even by much later tonight. Her cousin Judith called and she said she would drive over here but I'm afraid even Aurora might be too far away now. I wanted to call you so you could speak to her. At this point I'm not sure what consciousness she has left. She is unresponsive. Please understand that. But you can say whatever you would like to say. She can probably still hear every word. Okay? Are you ready?"

"Yes. Thank you."

Gloria put the phone receiver next to Violet Reynolds' left ear. Her son unplugged that stupid white USB cable and put his cellphone up against his own right ear.

"Mom!" he said.

He could think of nothing else to say at first. He could hear a gasp and he began to sob. He caught himself.

"I love you, Mom. It's okay. You don't have to fight anymore." He chuckled as these words came out because the woman he knew as Mom never needed permission from anyone to do anything and least of all from her son. Maybe this presumptive and smart-aleck attitude on his part would inspire her to rally yet again out of sheer spite. I'll go whenever I decide to go so quit watching my clock for me. Got somewhere to be? So rude. He liked supposing this. "You've fought long enough, Mom. Rest now. Be with Dad. It's okay. I love you so much. Goodbye, Mom."

There was a significant pause and Gloria sensed the son was finished and she spoke into the receiver.

"Very good, sir. Anything else?"

"I don't think so. That was probably more than she wanted me to say. Ha!" A mixture of sobs and laughter and halting speech resulting from both at once. "Thank you for calling me. That was very kind. How does she look now?"

"About the same. Her rapid breathing is back. This could be her state for quite a while or she could go any minute. We're on God's timeline now."

"Haven't we always been? Thank you, Gloria."

The man driving the black SUV noticed an odd occurrence on the interstate ahead of him.

"Gloria, I have to go. Something is happening on the road here. Thanks and call me again if anything changes." He ended the call and dropped his phone into the passenger floorboard.

Coming directly at him was a set of high beams. This made no sense at all. One-way interstate with three lanes all heading north. These were southbound lights. What is happening? He scanned the scene and tried to make sense of the facts in hand. What is happening?

Red Flares in the Left Lane

The white dually crested the hill and made its way down the southbound lane hoping to help in any way possible but it was too late. The flashing lights told him that much and instantly. The 4x4 pickup truck heading south in the northbound lane could not be diverted. Vehicles had honked and flashed their lights and none of it mattered. One such vehicle was a black SUV with Louisiana plates. It was now parked on the center median off in the grass and its driver had exited the vehicle.

An inverted gold sportscar lay in the grassy median mangled and halfway recycled. There was no chance its occupants had survived. A nondescript sedan had also pulled onto the left shoulder. The driver and passenger were following the sportscar from a rehearsal dinner. The couple standing in the grass comprised the bridesmaid and her plus one. They were bent at the waist with devastation. Bride and groom still inside the crushed lead vehicle.

If only the trailer and the truck bed had been empty but they were not. On the contrary: both were heavy laden with obsolete appliances and the engine found the going uphill difficult and the nearest U-turn was three quarters of a mile further north. This rig hated inclines. In fact an incline had started this whole mess. The white dually and the trailer were never built for sprinting and today even less so than usual. So much weight owing to a haphazard collection of worthless and priceless objects taxing those magnificent eight cylinders and those hefty four wheels along that stout rear axle. They were all overmatched by patient and relentless gravity. But this frustration was cloaked vanity. No vehicle could have prevented this outcome save the 4X4 pickup itself. And that decision had begun to take irreversible shape some two hours prior.

The driver pulled the white dually onto the left shoulder near the black SUV and he exited his truck.

Emergency responders were already on the scene. How had they gotten there so soon? Red flares ignited and dropped onto the pavement were diverting traffic towards the furthermost right lane and were even encouraging traffic to use the right shoulder as a conduit for sliding past the wreckage. Rubberneckers slowed to gaze upon the spectacle nonetheless and they found plenty to satisfy the most morbid of curiosities. Cleanup would take several hours.

Overhead a hospital helicopter searched for a way to provide medevac assistance to the driver of the 4X4 pickup. He was no longer conscious but his was the only life yet hanging in the balance. First the jaws of life and then a basket descending from a winch and then a trip to the nearest emergency room. After seven hours of surgery and an extended stay in intensive care the driver of the 4X4 would learn that his vehicular manslaughter trial would commence in six months. Two counts.

An exceptional public defender would eventually secure a sentence of eight years in prison as penance for two soon-to-be newlyweds lost forever. After all they had been drinking also including the future groom behind the wheel. Lab reports and dinner guests under subpoena. Context is everything. The driver of the 4X4 pickup was out in five years and change and so ends his role in this story.

The two drivers from Louisiana stood in silence on the side of the grassy median. The man owning the black SUV had blood on his hands and on his arms and on his shirt. The other man noticed this.

"What happened?"

The man owning the black SUV looked at the other man.

"The blood, I mean."

He sighed heavily.

"I tried to get her out. The kid driving had no chance at all. Neither did she but I thought she might. She was still with us for a minute or two. Maybe more, maybe less. Window was out and I tried to pull her out that way. She was pinned. Bleeding out. She didn't make any sounds. I saw her go, I think." He started to sob. "Damn," he said. "How the hell?"

"Why did you stop?"

"What do you mean? What else could I do?"

"I don't know. Keep driving. This wasn't on you."

"What the hell does that have to do with anything? Why did you stop for that matter?"

"I always stop. It's what you do."

"Yeah. It is. Poor kids. Their friends up there too. It's awful."

The man owning the white dually thought about everything. The old noise was having a hard time catching up. Who was this guy after all? The noise had no answer. And why had he followed this apparently decent man all the way from Corsequette Louisiana to St. Louis Missouri? The noise made no guess.

"New Orleans fan. Louisiana plates. You're a long way from home, mister."

"Yeah. I was headed up to Chicago but I'm not anymore. Well, I am. I'm just not in the hurry I was in earlier this morning."

"Why is that?"

"Oh. I was headed up there to see my mom but I just got the call. I'll spare you. Anyway. I got to see to her things now. You get it."

"Yeah. I do. I'm from Louisiana too matter of fact. Heading to Chicago looking for work."

"No kidding. Lance." He extended his right hand. The other man stood there puzzled for two awkward seconds and then made a decision. He accepted the handshake.

"Gary. Good to meet you, Lance. Bad timing though."

"Bad everything. I don't know about you but I kinda need to pull off the road and figure out some things. You?"

"Yeah. You could say that."

"There's a diner up the road. Buy you a cup a coffee, Gary?"

"Um. Yeah. I guess. Sounds good."

Gary followed Lance through a U-turn and then down the offramp and into the parking lot of a national restaurant chain promising pancakes of global significance. But coffee was all either man could manage at present.

No Disposable Moments (Part Two)

Gary James Matthews was unloading his trailer at Gumtree Estates when the call came. There should have been enough material in this load to finish units 7-12. Unless he ran into some irregular angles and inefficient uses of space but that was unlikely. These apartments were comprised of exactly two floorplans and he had already encountered both and he knew many tricks besides.

His assistants Joey and Marco and he himself were rotating in pairs to lift the sheets of drywall from the trailer and into the nearest driveway. He had a system for everything. Order. Years spent on jobs exactly like this one taught him all he needed to know and he accepted no additional input from anyone. Why else would he bother to venture out on his own and incur all the overhead and the headaches if not to make his own decisions? He had earned his right to do things his way and this was his advantage. He could outbid other companies because they had not been paying attention. Slop in their systems. His way was most efficient, from the screws to the wallboard to the mud to the finish. All he needed was one or two or three solid hands who would do as they were told and ask no useless questions and simply accept the order of things. Joey and Marco supplied this well enough and so Gary kept them on and paid them. His two hands were taking their turn carrying sheets when Gary's cellphone rang. The number said Corsequette PD. That was odd.

Hopefully no one had broken into his shop. Vandals. Kids. Junkies looking for copper, as if drywallers have any of that laying around. Could have been anything. Gary had seen it all and had heard it all by now. He answered the call.

"This is Gary."

"Mr. Matthews?"

"Speaking. What can I do for you?"

"Sir, this is Officer Ben Thompson with CPD. I'm going to need you to come to Thomas and Oak. Immediately. Do you know where that is?"

"Well of course I do but I don't understand. I don't have any jobs over there and my shop is on Olive."

"Your shop, sir? Mr. Matthews this isn't a work call, I'm afraid. There's been an accident involving your wife and daughter. Please meet us here as quickly as you can. I'll be here. Thank you."

The world stopped right there and it stopped forever. It should have stopped an hour ago at breakfast but the world insisted on spinning on a bit longer. Now look at what was happening. But it couldn't really be happening, could it? He remembered that his wife's favorite grocery store sat on the corner of Thomas and Oak and what was clearly impossible became an undeniable fact. It could not be true but he knew it was true. And the officer had not told him to meet them at the hospital. He wanted him to drive to the accident itself. And the police were calling him instead of Rhonda calling him. All of these hints pointed only towards one agonizing conclusion. It could not be true but it had to be true. It was true. It could not be true. But it was though. It was true. He knew it was true.

Gary fumbled with the trailer hitch trying to unhook his white dually with his logo magnets on its doors from the trailer so he could drive a bit faster. He had hooked and unhooked this coupling thousands of times and could have done so while sleepwalking but now he was fumbling with it as if it were some new and highly technical contraption. He started sobbing and then he started screaming. Marco and Joey dropped their stack and ran to him. Marco shooed Gary's hands away from the hitch and completed the task. Joey was too afraid to ask what was wrong because he was the brighter of the two.

93

"I have to go," said Gary.

His workers nodded and had no idea what to do next. The white dually was gone and Gary nearly sideswiped a parked delivery van while rounding the corner. Reality disappeared en route. But it returned when Gary saw Rhonda's minivan spun onto the concrete median. The driver's door was completely caved in as was the passenger door behind it. A lawman stood in front of the vehicle holding his hat in both hands. Gary looked across the scene for any sign of comfort and found none. Not even the other driver survived and Gary had no one even to scream at. But he screamed anyway.

Traffic cameras indicated that Rhonda and Melissa were driving carefully and orderly and should have been completely safe. But a man driving a red SUV came through the intersection and there was no evidence that he had ever tapped his brakes at all. The toxicology report concluded no alcohol or other inhibiting substances affected his response time. But cellphone data did indicate the man was texting at roughly the time of impact. The accident was thus categorized as simple distracted driving. A disposable moment that could never be disposed of now. Everyone told Gary James Matthews how sorry they were and they said lots of other things that were equally useless.

Coffee and What Now?

Lance Reynolds exited his black SUV and walked into the restaurant but Gary James Matthews lingered inside his white dually for just a bit longer.

He opened his glove box with the revolver inside and he thought about the unconscious man in the helicopter heading towards some St. Louis hospital. He wondered how many people in that facility who were there under honest and shitty circumstances would now be bumped downward in the priority queue for the sake of saving this useless turd and helping him to hopefully become a ward of the state for the remainder of his days or at least the remainder of his useful days. He didn't even know what to root for. Death en route? Death on the table? Recovery and then a prolonged and traumatic and public stint through the court system followed by years of incarceration and finally death via shiv in the shower? Or maybe all of that minus the shiv but instead a post-incarceration life exiled back into public life with no way to earn a livable wage and a future in which all the people who once loved him had now summarily turned their backs on him and now he was alone and broke and hopefully racked with guilt and would never experience peace again and that would be exactly what he deserves for killing Rhonda and Melissa.

Rhonda and Melissa.

Gary began to sob. He again put his head on the steering wheel. He gave himself a minute. What was happening? What had been happening? Why was he here? Why was he about to sit at a table with this Lance and, after all of this, what were they supposed to talk about? Rhonda and Melissa were gone. Lance and the man in the helicopter couldn't fix that. And they didn't even cause that. And killing either of them would never fix that. And nothing was ever going to fix any of it. And he sobbed even heavier. It felt horrible and it also somehow felt better. Why did it feel better? Was it even okay to feel better? A stupid cup of coffee with a stranger. Fine. I'll have some coffee. With some guy named Lance in this dumb restaurant. And in Missouri, no less. Death in front and death behind and death all around and now coffee with some guy named Lance. Shit. Why not? Why the hell not?

Gary wiped his eyes with some napkins left over from Memphis and he pulled himself together. He thought about getting rid of his pistol forever. Throw it into a river off some bridge as he drove across it and never look back and that sounded perfect. But he knew he wouldn't end up doing anything like that. He shut the lid again. A heavy sigh. All was quiet now and quieter than just the usual ebb. Everything felt so much better than it had since before leaving Corsequette Louisiana. But Gary knew better than to get too carried away with his newfound peace. That old noise was patient.

Gary exited his white dually and he went inside the restaurant. Lance had taken a prime booth against a large window facing the lights of the offramp. Of course he had.

Gary was still catching up to several things. So was Lance, probably, but to a much lesser extent.

Lance waved Gary over. They nodded. A waitress that neither man regarded with any particular attention set two coffee cups on their table and filled them and also placed a saucer with single-serve creamer cups onto the table. These were left undisturbed.

She asked if they knew what they wanted and both men communicated their disinterest in food of any sort without using words and she departed their table still carrying the menus. Gary picked up the sugar and began stirring it into his cup. What to say indeed. Even Lance felt the awkward but he was the better skilled in pushing past these sorts of barriers and so Lance began and Gary was grateful.

"Damn. So terrible."

"Yeah," said Gary.

"Never seen anything like it in my life."

"I have." Gary noticed Lance had changed his shirt. Must have had one handy or had his bag handy or something. He was glad to see that as well. "Headed to Chicago, you say?"

"Mom's dying. Broken hip and other shit. You know. Thing is, I'm not gonna make it."

"No? What do you mean?"

"Yeah, they called right before this accident in fact. Put me on with her." There was a catch in Lance's voice. "They, uh... They weren't sure but they thought she could hear me. See. She went to sleep and they can't wake her up anymore. They've seen this before and they don't think she'll make it to the morning."

"Jesus, man. That sucks." Gary said it and he meant it. He believed Lance now and somehow he cared and he even felt sorry for him without disgust or without even pity and all of it was just so damn weird. "Are you sure we should be here right now? I mean shouldn't you be on the phone with her? Until she passes?"

"Um. Well. That would be nice, I guess. But I can't see doing that. It would take a nurse standing there holding a phone to mom's ear while I drive and that just doesn't seem right or fair. They have other patients. Anyway, I told my mom everything I could think to say so... It's not the same as being there, you know. But I guess it's the best I can do. I hope she gets it."

"You never know, hoss. Could be she'll rally. They do that. Might be you'll get up there tomorrow and she's still kicking around after all. Tough lady, your momma?"

Lance laughed. "You've no idea. Yeah. You're right. What the hell do they know? Might even be sitting up and bitching about her soup by the time I roll into town."

Now they both laughed a bit. And when that chuckle lost its steam the awkward returned to the airspace surrounding the table.

"What about you, Gary? Chasing work you say?"

"Yeah. In Chicago too as a matter of fact. And I'm also from Louisiana. Go figure."

"No kidding! Not Baton Rouge?"

"No. Corsequette. Anyway, I'm a drywaller and I've had a pretty rough stretch of luck for a while now. Looks like they always have work up near Chicago so I don't know. I guess I figured I'd pull up stakes and head off somewheres I've never been and just kinda start over. That make sense?"

"Yeah, it does."

"No, it don't." They both chuckled again. "But that's what I'm doing anyway. Got everything I own with me so I guess there's no turning back now."

"Damn. You know I really admire that. Just. Screw it! Start over somewhere else. Why not! I'd love to do that. Been thinking about something like that for the last three years or so but I can't afford to leave. You know. Even so I can't see myself continuing to do what I've been doing for much longer."

Gary managed a smile but there was nothing behind it.

"Where are you staying?"

"Haven't quite worked that out yet."

"Wow. You really are going for it, aren't ya!"

"If you wanna call it that, I guess."

Lance thought about it for a minute. No way.

"Gary. You're not a hoarder are you? Never mind. Okay. I don't know you at all, Gary. Could be you're an unhinged lunatic two clicks away from going postal and I have no idea what I'm getting myself into here!" One of them laughed. "But I don't think so. Pretty good at reading people. Anyway. I just had an idea."

"Oh really? Go on."

"See. My mom has this house. I need help emptying it anyway and that's gonna be a big job. No lie. But after that I have no idea what I'm gonna do with it. Needs some work. Might flip it, I don't know. Don't really want to. But either way I'm in no hurry. So. You have a trailer and all your stuff and you're still looking around. Trying to get settled. Meanwhile I got this empty house on my hands in Chicago and I really need to get back home to my family and my job. I don't know. Maybe we can help each other out. What do you think?"

Gray quit stirring his coffee. Take that, Betty.

Three Final Calls and One More After

Lance had left his cellphone inside his black SUV. He didn't even miss it until he got back inside his vehicle and saw it in the passenger floorboard where he had dropped it. Three calls had come in and had gone to voicemail. The first one was from Scott Shetland. He considered deleting it without listening to it, but screw it. Why not play the damn thing? Might be good for a chuckle at least. The bastard.

"Buddy! Hey! Just checking in to see how your dad's doing. Trying to get some ideal about what's going down. I'm sure it's fustrating but I hope things are going okay and he's making a full resuscitation. Or you know. Getting better at least. Yeah. If not though I'd like to extend my convalescence for your loss. Your pop was a great guy, Guy. So. I know you're out until Christmas. Made that clear, Buddy. I was just, uh... Just hoping you could maybe make a few calls from there. Just when you need a break from the stress or whatever. No I in... Remember? Yeah. Anyway, hit me back, Buddy. Hashtag Team SIZZLE. Later, Guy."

He deleted the message. Judith was next.

"Lance! Honey, they just called. I guess they couldn't get ahold of you. I'm sorry. I know you're driving. Your mom. She was a great woman. I loved her so much and I'm really gonna miss her. Um. We aren't going anywhere over the holidays so I can help you clean out her things. There are a few things I'd like the boys to have before other people pick over everything worth having. Maybe we can coordinate that and her services and some of that stuff over the next few days. Call me when you're in town. I love you."

Timing. If only Lance knew where he could buy her some. He deleted her message also. Gloria from Pleasant Latter Days Skilled Nursing was the third call. He knew all but the details now.

"Mr. Reynolds. This is Gloria from Pleasant Days. Your mother went peacefully a few minutes ago. I was in her room just before and then I had to step out and check on another resident and when I returned she was gone. I am so sorry for your loss, honey. If you can still come by tomorrow we can have her things ready for you. Please call us when you get this. Goodbye."

Lance was out of tears for now. He called his wife.

"Hi, sweetie. She's gone. I didn't make it."

"Oh, baby. I'm so sorry!" She started crying.

"Yeah. Me too. But I met a guy. Long story. I'll tell you later. Anyway. He might be moving into mom's place after we clean it out, so that's a load off my mind."

"Wait. What?"

"I know, trust me. It's crazy. I get it. I'll tell you all about it later. Once my head clears, you know. Gotta work stuff out with Pleasant Days first and that's enough to think about right now. But I don't know. I mean I don't know this guy from Adam. Name's Gary. Anyway I think he's had some tough breaks or something. Don't know the whole story yet. But I just have a feeling about this guy. Seems like a really good dude. Good soul. I think we can trust him. Talk to you tomorrow, honey. Love you."

Lance disconnected the call with his wife and headed towards his Tremendous 10 motel in northern St. Louis, complete with two queens and other deluxe accommodations. At least now he could sleep in. The worst was certainly behind him and how comforting a thought that was.

Christmas was yet ahead and he remembered how much his mom loved Christmas morning. The excitement and the joy and the presents and the mystery and the food and just all of it. Violet loved all of it so much. She almost seemed a different person on Christmas mornings. The memory made him smile. Maybe Jodi and the kids could fly up and they could all spend Christmas together in that old house in Chicago. And maybe he should take his time sorting through that old clutter and try to understand what Violet and Judith saw in all that stuff. Maybe heirlooms and memories and treasures were buried somewhere in those piles after all. Maybe he had missed something important and maybe his mom still had something new to teach him. And maybe it was time for Lance to really think about getting out of the copier industry for good. Bills or no bills. Look at Gary. There's a guy not trapped by anything at all. Total freedom. Maybe Lance just needed a new mentor. He could learn a thing or two from that guy.

Soon a new year would begin and that made Lance smile too. Suddenly there were all sorts of new possibilities.